THROUGH THE WITCHES STONE

—·—

SCOTT A. JOHNSON

TIMBER GHOST PRESS

Through the Witches Stone

by Scott A. Johnson

Copyright © 2023, Scott A. Johnson

Published by Timber Ghost Press

Printed in the United States of America

Edited by: Beverly Bernard

Cover Art and Design by: Don Noble of Rooster Republic Press

Interior Design: Timber Ghost Press

Print ISBN: 979-8-9855521-7-1

www.TimberGhostPress.com

CONTENTS

For Katie.

PART ONE

GRANDMA'S HOUSE

Come away, O human child!
To the waters and the wild
With a faery hand in hand,
For the world's more full of weeping than you can under-
stand.
From *The Stolen Child* by William Butler Yeats

CHAPTER ONE

Hadley lurched awake at the sound of tires on gravel. For a moment, she wasn't sure where she was. Too much green, too much open sky. It was certainly different from Austin's skyline. Instead of glass and steel buildings, wood and green bordered the road, ivy and grass. Puffy lazy clouds of cotton drifted by in a wide blue sea without a care in the world and replaced the perpetually gray sky of the city. The only place she knew, or had ever been, that held such infuriating calmness was Grandma's house.

"Can't I stay home? Or maybe with Meagan?"

"No," said Mom. "I asked Grandma to look after you. It's just for a few weeks. You'll survive."

"But Grandma doesn't have Wi-Fi."

"You'll live without Wi-Fi for a bit," said Mom with a smirk. "It'll be good for you to unplug for a while. Besides, Grandma's got lots of fun stuff planned."

"Like what?"

"Same kind of stuff I did when I was your age," said Mom.

"That means chores," said Hadley.

"Not all of it. When I was your age, summer was lots of fun.

"Kids my age don't like doing the same kind of stuff you did when you were my age," said Hadley.

"We'll see about that," said Mom.

"What about us?"

Hadley turned in her seat and glared at her brothers. Josh and Cole sat on opposite sides of the car but might well have just been mirrors of each other. The twins were more than identical. It was like they shared a brain.

"If I have to do it, you have to do it," said Hadley.

"You're too young just yet," said Mom to the boys. "But I'm sure Grandma has fun stuff for you to do too."

Too young for the boys definitely meant chores for her and playtime for them. Yet another thing that wasn't fair. Summer vacation was supposed to be spent in the glorious pursuit of no responsibilities. Days filled with beach lounging, video games, shopping, ice cream, and fun with friends—that was how it was supposed to be. But as the road turned rough and the trees grew closer together, Hadley's hope of summer vacation slipped further and further away.

"It's not going to be as bad as you think," said Mom. "Give it a chance. I bet you'll be surprised."

"I doubt it," she muttered as she turned back toward the window.

As the trees passed, her mind drifted. Dad wouldn't have made her go to Grandma's. In fact, if Dad were still alive, they'd be at home right now. Mom could go on her stupid business trip, and Dad would build a tent out of blankets in the living room of their apartment and make s'mores over candles while they watched scary movies after he put the boys to bed.

But Dad was gone.

The road through the trees continued until, above the treetops, a chimney stack appeared. The soot-marked red brick stood out as the single piece of human settlement in the woods. Sometimes it was, to her, a beacon. But other times, it only stood out to show her how lonely Grandma's house could be.

Another moment or two dragged by until the car came through the tree line into the great clearing that was Grandma's yard. The gigantic farmhouse loomed over the driveway like an angry old queen, once beautiful and still commanding of respect in her age. The tall pillars on the wide front porch held up the roof like soldiers guarding the place. No matter how often she visited, Hadley could never escape the feeling that the second- and third-floor windows watched her.

The car stopped, and Mom put it in park and killed the engine.

"Okay," she said. "Everybody out. Grab your bags and let's head inside."

The boys didn't hesitate as they unbuckled their seatbelts and slid out of the car. Hadley sat for a moment and stared. No Wi-Fi. No cellphone reception. Grandma didn't even have video games or, as far as she knew, a television. She was doomed to a summer of farm chores and boredom.

"C'mon," said Mom through the open door. "Grandma's waiting."

She looked toward the house and, as she expected, Grandma stood on the front porch, a broad smile on her wrinkled face. She looked just as she always did when Hadley visited, wore the same overalls, and had the same fly-away hair. Her eyes sparkled, and her face was genuine and kind. It wasn't that Hadley didn't love her grandmother. But visits were supposed to be brief, not last the entire summer. In fact, she'd never spent more than a few hours at Grandma's house before.

"Now that just *can't* be my granddaughter, can it?" squealed Grandma as she ambled down the front steps. "Good lord, child, you've grown! What's your mama been feeding you?"

"Hi, Grandma," said Hadley. She tried not to let her voice sound too disheartened.

"And where are my grandsons?"

Josh and Cole stepped out from behind the car in unison, bags in hand and smiles on their usually expressionless faces. They dutifully stepped to Grandma and hugged her.

"I'm so happy y'all are here. C'mon in. I've just finished making up your rooms."

Hadley let out a heavy sigh as she trudged to the back of the car and removed her suitcase. Mom's sat right beside it, black and important looking. Hadley's was pink and covered in stickers. A child's suitcase. But she wasn't a child anymore. She was twelve years old, practically a teenager, and far beyond needing her grandmother to babysit her. Mom's suitcase looked boring by comparison, but it was bigger and could hold more stuff. It seemed more mature. At least that much she envied.

As she made her way to the porch, the old feeling of the windows watching her grew stronger. She looked from side to side, behind and above, but nothing presented itself. She dismissed the feeling as being tired from the hour-plus drive to Grandma's house.

The scent of must and firewood just inside the door tickled her nose. Something rich and savory was cooking in the kitchen, and from the smell of it, some of Grandma's amazing cornbread was in the oven as well. A few deep breaths was all it took to put her at ease. It was still going to be a boring summer, but at least she had Grandma's cooking to soothe the ache for technology.

The living room's dark wood walls and rich leather furniture gave the place the look of a hunting lodge. The oxblood easy chair sat where it had for all of her memories, by the fireplace, next to the matching couch. On the mantle sat photos of Mom sitting at the same fireplace as a little girl. In fact, nothing of Mom's childhood home ever seemed to change, and that was just the way Grandma liked it.

To one side was the doorway to the kitchen. On the other was the parlor with antique furniture too fancy to sit on and lace doilies she still didn't understand the purpose of.

The "Harvest Gold" walls of the kitchen seemed just as bright and inviting as they always did, with not a speck of dirt or grease on them from the years of cooking Grandma did. And the old mahogany table had no marks on the top, despite there never being a tablecloth Hadley could remember. Grandma's pans hung from a circular rack over the island, and her cast iron pots stayed under the cabinets when they weren't in use. Two were on the stove bubbling.

"We've got beef stew tonight," said Grandma with a smile. "Cornbread's in the oven, too."

"I can't stay," said Mom. "I should be—"

"You're staying," said Grandma. "Don't think you're too old for me to tan your butt, young missy."

Hadley giggled. Grandma was the only person on Earth who could talk to Mom with such authority and get away with it, too. To her credit, Mom knew she'd been beaten.

"Fine," she said. "But I can't be too long. I have to get back on the road. There's a long drive ahead of me."

"All the more reason you need a full stomach," said Grandma. "Okay kids. Upstairs! Straight to the third floor. Your rooms are ready."

The boys nodded in unison, a thing that never ceased to creep Hadley out, and bounded up the stairs. Hadley followed close behind, with Grandma and Mom bringing up the rear. The dark wooden stairs creaked as they climbed past the ornately carved posts.

"I don't use the stairs much anymore," said Grandma. "My hips don't like climbing like they used to. Moved my bedroom down to right behind the kitchen."

The stairs turned on the second floor before continuing to the third.

"Hold up!" said Grandma from the stairwell. "Before you go up, I need to tell you something."

The boys stopped and waited while Hadley took in her surroundings. She'd seen the floor before, of course. There were old photographs on the walls, yellowed in their dark ornamental frames. The three doors on the floor always held mystery for her, though, as she'd never known what behind each one.

"First rule," said Grandma, a little out of breath. "Y'all are welcome anywhere in the house, but don't go opening up any locked rooms. We keep 'em locked for a reason and don't need nobody in 'em. Clear?"

"Yes, Grandma," said Hadley.

"And while we're at it," she continued. "There're two more rules you need to follow. Second rule, don't go inviting anyone I don't know into the house. And third, stay out of the woods. Them woods is dangerous, and I don't need none of you getting lost. Think you can handle that?"

"Yes, Grandma," said Hadley. The boys nodded then ran up the next set of stairs.

At the top of the landing, they stopped. Three more doors greeted them—left, center, and right—that she'd never been through before.

"Boys," said Grandma from below. "To the left."

Hadley followed as they pushed the door open. The room inside was unlike the rest of the house in that the colors were light, the furniture fit for children. There were two beds, side by side, each done up with a comforter covered in trains and boats and planes. Between them, light streamed through a large window. It was a nice room, larger than the one they shared at home.

"How's that suit y'all?" Grandma stood in the doorway, beaming.

The boys smiled and nodded and then put their suitcases on their beds. Somehow, they were in total agreement about which bed belonged to whom and about who was doing what. They always seemed to be in agreement without speaking, and no one ever saw one without the other. If she hadn't grown up used to it, she supposed she might find it weird.

"Take a look in the middle door," said Grandma.

Hadley turned the knob and pushed. The bathroom inside looked modern, with a stand-up shower, toilet, and dual sink area.

"That's for the boys," said Grandma. "Yours is over there." She jabbed a thumb toward the third door. "Go take a look."

The boys' room was large and nice, but it was plain, perfect for Josh and Cole, but not at all to her liking. Grandma went through obvious pains to make sure everything was nice for them, so, she told herself, no matter what lay beyond the door, she was going to be nice about it. She took the knob and pushed.

The room beyond was enormous. Light colors and fabrics dominated the walls, and a queen-sized bed sat on a platform at the far end of the room. Against a wall sat a vanity next to another door.

"That's your bathroom," said Grandma, her eyes sparkling. "Young lady needs her own bathroom, to my mind."

Hadley hurried to the door and opened it. Inside, she found a spacious room with a clawfoot tub, a small bench, a sink and mirror, and toilet. The room was painted in shades of purple and blue, gold and green.

"It's beautiful," said Hadley.

"Isn't this the master bedroom?" Mom crossed her arms and cocked an eyebrow.

"Not anymore," said Grandma. "Not since this damned hip of mine. Now it's Hadley's room. And she ain't even seen the best part. Go look over there."

Hadley followed the line of Grandma's finger to a set of French doors on the wall. When she opened them, the view stole the air from her lungs.

The doors led to the balcony she'd seen from below. On it, a chaise sat with a small table.

"You can see the whole yard from up here," said Grandma. "This was my favorite place for reading."

"I can see why," said Hadley. A breeze tossed her hair and licked her face.

"What do you think?" Mom stood behind Grandma in the room. "Will this work for you?"

"It's perfect," said Hadley as she hugged Grandma tight. Summer might not work out the way she'd wanted, but at least it would be comfortable.

"Good," said Grandma. "Now put your stuff down and come get dinner."

Grandma's stew was no run-of-the-mill recipe. The thick broth contained chunks of carrot and potatoes, but also had a mixture of beef, lamb, and rabbit to give it a flavor unique to Grandma's kitchen. The more she ate, the more Hadley loved it. Grandma's cornbread was sweet and buttery, just the way she liked it.

After a single bowl, Mom declared herself stuffed, gave a round of kisses and hugs, then made the boys promise to be good as she hurried out to the car.

"Watch after your brothers," said Mom. There was an edge to her voice that sounded like real fear, but she smiled as she headed out the door.

Hadley stood and watched as the brake lights disappeared down the gravel road. When she couldn't see their red glow in the dust anymore, it finally hit her. Mom was gone. Summer was going to be spent at Grandma's. No friends, no phone, no games. She had books and her brothers to keep her occupied, and whatever chores Grandma had planned. But days of shopping and ice cream and swimming pools seemed out of reach.

"Did I miss her?" Grandpa burst in through the back door, his beard a mess of twigs and sawdust, his grey hair askew beneath his snap-back hat.

"Afraid so," said Grandma. "Said she had to go. Got a long drive ahead of her."

"Aw," said Grandpa. "Wish she'd have stayed around just a little bit longer."

"Where were you?" Hadley caught her grandfather in a bear hug.

"Out in the barn," he said. "Couldn't leave the work half done, y'know? Work don't tend to itself."

"I bet Mom would've stayed if she'd known you were here."

Grandpa's face turned sad for a moment.

"Maybe," he said. "Your old Grandpa did something a while ago that your momma didn't like. And now... Well... She just won't see me."

"You think she left without seeing you on purpose?"

Grandpa nodded then took a deep breath.

"Something smells good," he said through a broad smile. "Is that stew?"

"It is," said Grandma. "And you can help yourself, on account of you missed dinner with the rest of us. Get these boys to help you clean up, too. Me and Miss Hadley need to get busy."

"Doing what?" Josh stood up from the table, his interest piqued. "Whatever Hadley's doing, count us in!"

"You're too young yet," said Grandpa. "Best you two give me a hand cleaning up."

The boys groaned their displeasure, and Grandma took Hadley by the hand and led her out of the kitchen and into the parlor. Maybe Grandma wanted to teach her how to crochet doilies, or maybe teach her how to properly dust.

For as long as she could remember, Grandma had never used the parlor. On visits, Mom always told her to stay out of the special room. The furniture was too old, she'd said, or too expensive. It was to look at, not to use. The phrase struck Hadley as ridiculous. Why have furniture if no one could use it? But as Grandma took her into the room, she gave it her first really good look.

The two high-backed chairs were made of some dark wood with intricately embroidered cloth pillows for seats. The couch was the same, though Grandma called it a loveseat. Next to it stood a small table with a marble top and a pink frosted glass lamp. Grandma pulled a long match from the drawer below it and struck it. As the match flared, she noticed other things around the room that the darkness had concealed. More photographs on the wall, but also a cabinet she'd never seen before. On top of it were two books, candles, a bell, and two statues. One was a beautiful woman in a flowing gown. The other was a man with deer horns atop his head. Between the books, a long double-edged knife sat.

Grandma ushered her into the room then sat in one of the too-good-for-sitting chairs and gestured for Hadley to sit in the other.

"You're old enough," said Grandma. "And it's high time. Your mama wanted me to start your lessons this summer, and I've agreed to teach you, just like I taught her. Just like my momma taught me."

Bad enough that there was to be no real summer vacation, but school? Lessons? That was the last straw. She'd never forgive her mother for making her study over the summer break, even one day. If she thought Grandma was going to make her study boring subjects for the entire summer—

"Tell me," said Grandma. "Did your mama ever tell you that you come from a long line of witches?"

CHAPTER TWO

It took her almost a full minute to register what Grandma had said. Witches. She couldn't be serious. Could she? She certainly seemed serious. But witches weren't real. Witches only existed in movies and television and fairy tales, not in the modern world of cars and computers and online shopping. They wore black pointed hats and had warty noses, green skin, and rode around on broomsticks. She had to be joking.

"I'm not joking," said Grandma. "It's high time you learn the real way of things. There's so much more to the world than you know. When I was your age, my mother taught me to obey the laws of nature and how to use magic. *Real* magic. When your mama was your age, I taught her, same as I was taught. And now I've offered to teach you as well."

"Mom knows magic?" It was ridiculous. Mom was about as magical as a pair of socks.

"She does." Grandma nodded. "But she doesn't use it anymore. Lost her spark somewhere. But you, you still got it. And I figure some day you could have stronger magic than your momma ever did. Or even me. What d'you say?"

Hadley didn't know what to say. She didn't even really know what it meant to be a witch, or what kind of magic she meant. But more, it was something she could do and her brothers couldn't. They weren't old enough yet, which meant Grandma would be all hers for her lessons.

"What kinds of things can witches do?"

Grandma's sparkling eyes narrowed and her smile widened.

"All manner of things. Things you can imagine and things you can't. You just wait and see," she said. "So, does that mean you want to learn? Because I can't teach you if you don't want to learn. That's one of our rules."

"I need a minute," she said. "This is a lot."

"Take your time," said Grandma. "But don't dally. I gots lots to teach you, and I ain't got buckets of time to do it in."

Hadley went out onto the front porch and sat in the old swing. Witches. Magic. What did that mean about her family? What did that mean about her? Did she really have powers? Could she have powers? What if it was a game, some little kiddie game that Grandma was playing because she couldn't see Hadley for how old she really was. But then, what if it wasn't?

How had her mother kept it from her for twelve years? And why had she kept it from her? Surely, there'd been signs, but she'd been too young to notice them, she supposed. And how had Mom lost her spark?

That one, she might have an answer to. Maybe she lost it when Daddy died. If so, maybe her spark was gone too.

If what Grandma said was true, if she came from a long line of witches, it made her special, made her family special.

Her decision made, Hadley got up and marched back into the house. Grandma still sat in the parlor, a crooked smile on her lips, like she knew all along what Hadley would decide.

"How many witches are there?" Hadley took her seat again.

"Not many," said Grandma. "Not many at all. That's why it's important to pass the learning down, so we can keep the spark alive. Do you want to learn?"

"Yes," said Hadley. "I think I do."

"Good!" said Grandma. "Now. We need a pact. Give me your right hand. Right-hand promises can't be broken."

Hadley did as she was told, and Grandma took a soft piece of rope from out of her overalls, then she grasped

Hadley's hand. Grandma wrapped their hands in the rope.

"Now," she said. "I promise to teach you the lessons as I learned 'em as best as I can. You must promise to learn the best you can. Deal?"

"Deal."

"Good!" Grandma grasped her hands and shook them. It might've been her imagination, but for a moment, the rope gave off a faint blue glow and then dropped to the floor.

"When do we start?"

"Right now!" Grandma guided her off the chair to the strange cabinet with the statues at the wall. "The first thing you need to know is that we live by a single law. Well, we live by many rules and laws, but there's one that trumps them all. *An it harm none, do as thou wilt*. Repeat it."

Hadley did as she was instructed.

"We call that *The Rede.* It means as long as we ain't hurting nobody, we can pretty much do as we want."

"That sounds good," said Hadley.

"It does, don't it? There's more to it than that," said Grandma. "But for now, we'll leave it at that."

"Who are they?" Hadley gestured toward the statues.

"We'll get to them," said Grandma. "But first, I want you to have this."

She opened the cabinet and pulled out a book. The cover was covered in strange symbols tooled into the leather. Hadley turned the latch and opened the cover. The pages were blank and of a type of paper she'd never seen or felt.

"I made this for you," said Grandma. "This is to be your *grimoire*. Think of it as a journal of your journey into magic. The pages are cotton, and I tooled the cover myself."

"What do I put in it?"

"Spells. Thoughts. Anything, really," said Grandma. "The point is to write down what you learn so you can pass it on later. Also, so you know what works for you and what doesn't. We're all different, so nothing works for just everyone."

"Josh and Cole..."

"They ain't old enough yet," said Grandma. "But when they are, I'll teach them too. Or your mother will. Or maybe you will. Now, off to bed with you. Tomorrow starts your lessons."

"This isn't a game, is it?"

Grandma's eyes sparkled as she raised a hand. The flame from the top of the lamp danced and spat, then leaped off the wick and touched down on the tip of Grandma's finger, where it flickered in place.

"Everything's a game," said Grandma. "If you believe it to be. That don't make it any less real."

It was a lot to take in, but Hadley lay on her bed in the dark and tried to make sense of it all. Maybe Grandma was crazy. But then again, Hadley couldn't explain the trick with the lamp fire, so maybe she wasn't crazy. She'd always wanted to feel special in some way. The grimoire was smooth under her fingers, cool to the touch. She lifted the latch on the cover and opened it to the first page. For some reason, it seemed wrong to write in such a thing with a ballpoint pen, but it was all she had. She'd have to ask Grandma about it tomorrow.

At the top of the page, she put the date. Then, after a bit of consideration, she decided on the first line she would write.

This is the magical journey of Hadley Annette Bishop.

She looked at the page, then satisfied, she closed the book and the latch.

She should've been tired, and her body was. But her mind wouldn't stop racing at the possibility of what it meant to be a witch, what it meant to know magic. Surely, she wouldn't be able to do things like cast love spells or turn mean little boys into toads. That sort of thing only happened in movies, she was certain. Of course, an hour ago she was certain that witches only existed in movies, so who was to say?

Rather than lay in bed without sleeping, Hadley got up and went to the French doors, opened them, and stepped out onto the balcony. The moon shone bright and huge in the night sky, bathing the yard below in silver. Even though it was late, it surprised her how well she could see the yard to the tree line. For a moment she sat, not really watching or expecting anything to happen, but thinking about the new direction her life had gone.

A sound from below pulled her attention. The bushes and grass rustled, and a herd of deer emerged from the tree line. In front, a large buck with impressive antlers sniffed the air, then nodded, and the rest came out. There were three without antlers, girls Hadley guessed, and six that were smaller, babies. As she watched, more creatures came out of the woods to stand in the moonlit yard. Skunks, opossums, and several that she didn't know their names broke the tree line and stopped at the trough that grandpa kept full of water by the barn.

Hadley sat and watched, entranced. She'd never seen deer so close before. Possums, yes, but never deer. And she'd always been taught to be afraid of skunks, but those below her were beautiful and waddled like cats that had eaten too much. As she watched, another rustle came from the tree line, but instead of an animal, she was shocked to see a little girl step out of the shadows.

From where she sat, the girl was too far away for Hadley to see her too clearly. But her white dress glowed in the moonlight, and she looked to be right around Hadley's age.

The girl went from animal to animal, petting each of them for a moment before moving on, then went to the big buck at the front of the group. As she scratched its ears, the girl looked up. Her eyes and Hadley's locked, then she smiled and darted back into the woods. The rest of the animals followed and, a moment later, the yard was empty.

"Draw in your breath," said Grandma. "And focus."

Hadley did as she was told and stared at the pile of twigs in the ring until her eyes bulged and her head throbbed, but nothing happened.

"You have to feel the energy flowing into the wood."

"But where does the energy come from?" Hadley's vision blurred, then she blinked and looked up at Grandma.

There was no disappointment in her face. Only love and patience.

"All around," said Grandma. "You can either push it from inside of you or pull it from something else."

"Like what?"

"Plants," she said. "Animals. Anything alive has it. But you have to be careful. You pull too much out of a plant..."

She reached out and touched the leaf of a daffodil. Under her finger, the flower wilted, turned brown, then dried out.

"You killed it," said Hadley.

"Yes," said Grandma. "That's what happens. Same thing with animals and people. That's why we don't draw power from them unless we have to. But you also have to be careful of pushing too much of yours. Push too much energy out of yourself..."

"You could die," said Hadley as she turned her eyes back to the twigs.

"Yes," said Grandma. "That's why we use magic sparingly, and only when it's really important."

"I understand." She closed her eyes and concentrated.

"All your energy comes from here." Grandma's hand touched her stomach. "It's your center. It's like water in your belly, and it swirls around like a whirlpool. Now picture it in your mind."

Hadley did as she was told, a great swirl of water that churned and raged.

"When you got it," said Grandma, "picture it flowing down your arms like a river."

Hadley focused until the image of the whirlpool was clear, then she pushed the water in a tiny trickle through her arm and onto the twigs. When she opened her eyes, smoke rose from the tiny bundle.

"There!" said Grandma. "Keep going! Set it on fire!"

In the joy of the moment, Hadley's concentration shattered, and the smoke dwindled to nothing.

"Crap!" She threw her hands up and looked to her Grandmother.

"You almost had it," she said. "Not bad. It takes practice. Just be patient and it'll come."

From across the yard, one of the boys whooped. Hadley raised her eyes to see a small pile of wood, fire proudly flickering above it, with the boys dancing around in a circle. Of course, they did it first. They were too young to learn about magic, but somehow they could still use it. And they *still* outshone her. Maybe they had a natural ability, or maybe it was because they were just weird. Whatever the cause, their success enraged her. It was supposed to be *her* time with Grandma. *Her* time to be the special one. They got all the attention at home because they were twins and acted like weirdos. No one ever really even seemed to care what Hadley was up to, not when her brothers were around.

"Don't you pay them no mind," said Grandma. "Beginner's luck, I say. Don't you worry. You'll have more magic in your pocket by the time summer's over than those two will have in their whole bodies. I promise."

It made her feel a little better. Not much, but enough that the anger settled into dull annoyance.

"Grandma, do you have any neighbors?"

"Not for about five miles in any direction," said Grandma. "Why?"

"I was awake last night," she said. "I watched animals come into the yard, and then there was this girl—"

"What girl?"

"Just a little girl," said Hadley. "She was wearing a white dress and had blond hair. She petted all the animals, then she ran back into the woods."

"You probably just dreamed it," said Grandma. "Ain't no girls around here. You and your brothers are the only kids around for miles. That's how I like it. Makes it easier to teach you what I need to teach you."

"I wasn't dreaming."

"Well," said Grandma. "Even if you weren't, best to leave her alone. I don't much like strangers, and I like folks trespassing on my property even less."

"Yes, ma'am," she said.

"Now, you stay here and practice," said Grandma. "I need to go help Grandpa, then I need to make lunch. After lunch, I'll teach you about some of the wild plants around here and what we can do with them."

Grandma pushed herself slowly to her feet then ambled toward the house. When she reached the back door, she turned back and scanned the yard, then gave Hadley a brief smile and went inside.

Something was wrong. It wasn't like Grandma to be so evasive. She knew something about the little girl. She had to. So why wouldn't she tell her? The chance to have someone her own age around, another girl just like her, was too good to pass up. She loved her brothers, like any sister would. But they always had each other, shared their own private jokes, even seemed to speak their own language at times. More and more, whenever she was with them, she felt alone. She wanted a friend, a sister even, to share her days with. Grandma didn't even ask, didn't even care about her feelings on it. She was just a stranger. But didn't everyone start out as strangers? Everyone she'd ever met was a stranger until she'd put out a hand and said hello. Grandma was just being silly.

She glared at the little bundle of twigs that wouldn't light. The boys got theirs to light, even without Grandma teaching them how. And they celebrated together and left her out, just like she always felt left out.

"Just *burn*," she yelled. At her word, the kindling burst into flame and was reduced to ash in a matter of seconds. The flash was bright enough to knock her backward and to attract the attention of her brothers, who ran over to see what had happened.

"I'm fine," she said as she brushed their hands away and struggled to sit up. The place where the kindling had been was just a giant black scorch on the lawn, and her gut gnawed at her like she'd not eaten in days. But she'd done it. She didn't know how exactly, but she'd done it, and that was a start.

Grandma emerged from the back door and smiled.

"Saw it," she said. "Good job. Gonna have to teach you some control next. And I'll bet you're hungry, huh? Figured you would be, after a blast like that. C'mon. Lunch is almost ready."

It was the best statement she'd heard all day.

CHAPTER THREE

L unch consisted of grilled cheese sandwiches made on Grandma's home-baked sourdough bread and tomato soup cooked with tomatoes from Grandpa's garden. Grandma also served lemonade, made with lemons from the tree in her yard. As soon as the first bite touched her stomach, the pangs went away and she felt the strength return to her body.

"Magic is hungry work," said Grandma with a wink. "You pull the energy from your body, you have put it back. And that means food. Now. I have to go into town for a couple of hours. Can you look after your brothers while Grandpa and I go run some errands?"

"How long?"

"Not long," said Grandma. "While I'm gone, you can try to figure out how you blew them sticks up. If you've got it down by the time I get back, I'll teach you something new."

"Okay," she said. Watching her brothers wasn't her idea of a good time, but if Grandma needed the help, it was the least she could do. Besides, the boys always napped after lunch. Maybe they would leave her alone and let her practice in peace for a while.

After the dishes were done and put away, Grandma and Grandpa climbed into the ancient pickup truck and trundled off down the driveway. When the brake lights were no longer in sight, Hadley let out a long sigh.

Josh and Cole went down for their nap without a fuss, though they stared at each other in silent wide-eyed communication. She closed the door and let out a heavy breath.

The summer wasn't at all what she'd expected. Mom said she'd be surprised, and she was right. But for everything that was fun, there were still little things that were difficult. Learning magic, for example, was interesting. Frustrating, but interesting. The rules of energy and how to push power from one thing into another were complex. But Grandma's rules about who could and who couldn't come into the house were strange. To have such a rule when the only other person she'd seen was a girl in the middle of the night made no sense. And it would've been great to have a friend. She was learning fun stuff, sure, but she was still lonely.

Hadley took the stairs to the second floor slowly, almost at a trudge. Her sour mood didn't seem to be something a book could lift. All she really wanted to do was find the little girl and talk to her. Maybe ask her about how she got so close to the deer. But, again, Grandma wouldn't talk about her. Another of Grandma's strange and pointless rules.

As she came to the landing on the second floor, she glanced about to the three doors. Locked, all of them. Yet another rule without reason. Stay out of the rooms with locked doors.

If Grandma hadn't mentioned it, Hadley wouldn't have thought about them. Locked doors were just locked doors. Until, of course, someone told her not to go in. Then questions formed in her mind. Why were they locked? Didn't she know that locking the doors only made her want to know what was in them even more? Was Grandma hiding something in the rooms? And if so, what could she possibly be hiding? By telling Hadley to stay away from them in such a strong manner, she'd practically invited her to try to see what was in them.

Hadley walked slowly to the first door and tried the knob. It wouldn't turn, and no matter how hard she pressed her shoulder against the door, it wouldn't budge.

The second door was the same, locked tight and firm in the jamb.

She came to the third door and gave the knob a half-hearted brush with her fingers. To her surprise, it turned. She took hold and gave it a good forceful twist. The door clicked and creaked open.

Dust motes drifted in the stagnant air, hung motionless in the sunlight that filtered in through gauze curtains. It was darker than the rest of the house, but not so dark she couldn't see. There was a small bed, a dresser, a desk, and even a vanity. And atop every piece of furniture sat knick-knacks and keepsakes that gave clues to the identity of the room's one-time owner. It was a girl's room, and it was no stretch to figure who the girl was.

Mom, when she was about Hadley's age.

She stepped into the room, careful not to make a sound or disturb anything. Although, if she did, who would know? Grandma and Grandpa were gone, and the boys were asleep, or at least pretending to be asleep, so who would know if she poked around in Mom's old room? Besides, she could only imagine what she might find, what sort of insight she might gain into her mother at her age. Did she really never do the things she said she didn't do at her age? Did she really enjoy playing outside? Was she as good at magic as Grandma said? What made the little girl with the lacy curtains and horse figurines turn into... well... Mom?

Atop the dresser were photos framed in steel and glass, plastic and popsicle sticks. Younger Grandma and Grandpa, when their names were Mom and Dad, stood beside a gap-toothed Mom with a fish on a string. Another showed Mom in a one-piece swimsuit at the Blanco river. The third photo wasn't in a frame, but just sat on the dresser top. She picked it up and blew dust off, then squinted to see the image in the pale light. The image made her pause then sent a thrill of wonder down her back. There was a second girl in the photo, one who looked very much like the girl she'd seen in the yard last night, arms around Grandma and Grandpa and Mom. The old farmhouse stood in the background, less worn. Hadley turned the photo over. On the back was written "Megan, Patricia, Carl, Whilma, 1979."

Megan was Mom, Carl and Whilma were Grandpa and Grandma, so who was Patricia? She must've been a friend of the family, maybe Mom's best friend when she was growing up. Maybe the little girl in the yard was her daughter. But if that had been the case, why would Grandma not want to talk about her?

Around the room were more photographs similar to the ones on the dresser. In each of them, the subjects changed, but the two constants were always Mom and Patricia. By the bed was one silver picture frame with a photo of just the two of them. At the bottom of the frame, a single word was etched.

"Sisters."

How could Mom have a sister she didn't know about? It didn't make sense.

The rest of the furniture held ribbons and bows, certificates and knick-knacks. One of them was a small smooth river stone with a hole through the center. Hadley liked it, so she picked it up and put it in her pocket for later examination.

Mom seemed to have had a thing for horses, as Hadley found dozens of them scattered throughout the room. When she came to the desk, she stopped. On top, covered in dust, was a leather-bound book marked "Diary." She gingerly opened the cover. On the first page was printed "This Diary Belongs To" with her mother's name scrawled across the blank.

Hadley tucked the diary under her arm, then took one more look around the room to make sure she'd left nothing else out of place. It would be smarter to take it back to her room to read it rather than risk being caught somewhere she wasn't supposed to be. She pulled the door shut behind her and hurried up to her room.

As she passed the boys' room, she paused. There were no sounds. Good, because it meant they weren't talking. But there was also none of the tell-tale snoring she always heard when the two of them napped. They weren't asleep. She just hoped they didn't hear her in Mom's old room. She crept past their door and into her room, then closed the door as quietly as she could. Then, she lay on the bed and opened the diary and began to read.

The first few entries were brief, paragraphs about her new diary and how Mom was going to document her life because of how amazing it was going to be. She wrote entries about Grandma being a witch, and about how she was training in magic as well. The first one spoke of the same first lesson Hadley had, and how Mom had just as much trouble getting the sticks to light. To know her mother found it difficult, too, somehow made her feel better. Some of the entries spoke of a particularly difficult spell or about how some plants didn't react the way she thought they should've. It was strange to think of her mother at her age, learning from Grandma the way she was doing. The person in the diary seemed excited by magic, full of adventure and wonder. A completely different person than the mother who took business trips and fussed over bills. Whatever could have made the one into the other?

A few entries talked about boys she liked, and it seemed wrong of Hadley to read those entries. But most of them talked about playing in the woods and learning magic. And many of them mentioned Patricia, her sister.

Patricia was younger by at least a couple of years, though it never said exactly how many. And, like any younger brother or sister, she was annoying. Almost every entry had at least one line about something dumb Patricia did or something that Patricia ruined. The words didn't sound mean or hateful, but tired. Mom wanted to play in the woods, but Patricia was afraid. Mom wanted to practice magic, but Patricia said they should wait on Grandma. Mom wanted to be left alone to read, but Patricia was always nearby and underfoot.

Two entries in particular caught Hadley's eye.

July 4, 1979 – We spent the day floating the river. Patricia whined the whole time. When the time for fireworks came, she cried at the loud booms and bright lights. I wish she'd just go away.

July 5, 1979 – I didn't mean it. I swear, I didn't mean it. She ran off into the woods. Mom and Dad can't find her. I can't find her. I was supposed to be watching, but she was underfoot and I just wanted to read. And now she's gone. She's got to come home. I miss my sister. I'm so sorry.

Hadley closed the book and stared at the ceiling. How many times had she had the same thoughts about her brothers, just wished they'd go away? And what would she do if one day they just disappeared? Would it be her fault for wishing them gone? Magic was, after all, making wishes come true, wasn't it? No wonder she'd never spoken about her. Patricia had disappeared when Mom was just a kid. And it was obvious Mom blamed herself.

But if that were true, if the child in the picture disappeared, who was the little girl in the yard?

CHAPTER FOUR

As much as she wanted to ask Grandma, she didn't dare. There was no way to explain how she'd even heard the name, unless she were to admit she went snooping where she wasn't allowed. The same was true for Grandpa, although there was less opportunity to ask him, seeing as he spent all his time out in the barn. She didn't know exactly what he did out there, but Grandma always told her never mind and to keep her attention on her studies.

It seemed to her the best way to find out what was going on was to just ask the little girl herself, if she saw her again.

"We know what you're doing," said Cole. He and Josh had been playing by the barn while Hadley was still trying to get the stick to light consistently.

"What're you talking about?"

"We know you took Mom's diary from the room," said Josh. "That's bad."

"Did not," she said, even though it was pointless. They knew. They always knew. It was one of the things about them that made other people uncomfortable. To her, it was just an annoyance.

"Don't worry," said Cole. "We won't tell."

"We just don't think you should wait for her is all," said Josh.

"Wait for who?" They couldn't have seen the little girl. Their window faced the other side of the house.

"We have a bad feeling about her," said Cole.

"You two are being silly," she said. "Go play. Grandma and Grandpa will be home any minute now."

"They're coming up the driveway now," said Josh. "They brought ice cream for after dinner." He smiled.

"How do you know that?"

"Dunno." They both shrugged. That was always their answer when they didn't want to answer, like when they thought the answer might be scary to some people. Their "dunno" always meant more than it let on.

"Great," said Hadley. She'd lost her taste for ice cream since her father died. In fact, every time she saw a carton, it made her sad. The sight of one type in particular made her cry every time. "Watch this."

She cleared her mind and focused on the pile of sticks in front of her. In her mind's eye, the energy of her body swirled like water around her middle and then flowed out of her core, down her arm, and into the small pile of sticks. After a moment, the kindling smoked then burst into flames.

"I did it!"

The two didn't say anything but gave her placid smiles, then turned in unison and walked back toward the house. As they reached the back porch, the old truck trundled up the driveway. Grandma beeped the horn.

"I got ice cream for dessert," she shouted.

How did the boys know?

Once dinner was done, Hadley and the boys cleared the table and washed the dishes. The boys wolfed down big bowls of ice cream each. Hers remained untouched.

She hated the idea of doing dishes by hand because Grandma didn't have a dishwasher, but she had to admit it was nice that the boys helped by drying and putting the clean things away. She didn't feel so much like she was doing it all herself.

Grandpa sat on the couch with his newspaper while Grandma sat at the hearth with Hadley and continued her lessons.

"In magic," she said. "What you put out into the world comes back to you threefold. That means that if you're bad, bad stuff comes back to you. If you're good, good stuff happens to you."

"But what about when bad things happen to good people?"

Grandma smiled.

"That part's a nice old wives' tale, but that don't make it true. The truth is, that part of our beliefs is put there to encourage people to be good. Not like other systems where people say, 'be good or get punished.' We say you get what you give. Does that make sense?"

Hadley nodded. It was like Mom always told her to treat people the way she wanted to be treated. Most of the time, being nice to people made them nice back. There were bullies, it was true, but most of the time their bullying got them into more trouble.

"True or not," said Grandma. "It's a nice notion."

Grandma drew her book from behind her and motioned for Hadley to do the same.

"Write what you learned today," she said. "Write what it means to you. Years from now, you'll look back on it and see how far you've come."

Hadley glanced up at the window. It was dark outside.

"I'll write it in my room," she said. "Then I think I'll go to bed. I'm tired."

Grandma leaned closer and kissed her forehead.

"G'on then," she said. "Good dreams. So much more to do tomorrow."

Hadley lay in her bed and stared at the ceiling. Every so often, her eyelids drooped, but she fought sleep away. She wanted to see the girl, needed to find out who she was.

After a long while, the house went quiet except for the creaks and groans that came with age. She got out of bed and padded to the French doors, then opened them gently. They swung wide without a sound.

The moon wasn't quite at its highest point yet, the point when the girl first appeared. She still had time. A faint breeze blew across the balcony, and on it were lilacs and thistles, grass and wildflowers. She took a deep breath and held it as if doing so would keep Grandma's yard in her heart and lungs forever. Then she turned and exited her room as quietly as she could.

The stairs creaked. They always creaked. But since she'd decided to sneak out, Hadley made an effort to learn which steps were the worst. From the top, the fifth, the third, and the second steps made noise. All the steps let out a little groan, but the fifth, third, and second steps sounded like someone stepping on a cat's tail if they were hit just right. She made it to the second floor without so much as a whisper. All she had to do was make it through the mine-field of the stairs to the first floor. Where there were only three really bad steps on the previous flight, the second flight seemed designed to set off alarms to keep children in bed. There was a loose board on the landing, and steps fifteen, twelve, ten, and six all let out horrible caterwauls if stepped on. But the other steps were the most dangerous. Not because they were broken or anything, but because they let out noises seemingly at random.

The trick, however, was to walk not *on* the steps, but *beside* them on the part where the railing met the floor. She had to put her feet between the rungs and side-step down to avoid the noise, but it was worth it when she arrived on the first floor without a single squeak.

Then she padded across the living room, through the kitchen, to the back door, and made her way out into the moonlight.

From her balcony, the yard was a pool of silver where everything could be seen. But from the grass, it was still dark. Things that were familiar in the daytime took on sinister dark looks and stayed just out of clear eyesight, no matter how close she moved to them.

Hadley moved to the spot where she could see her balcony, where she figured the little girl had been the night before, then hid behind the porch and watched. After a few minutes, she began to feel a little foolish. There was nothing that said the little girl came every night. There was no reason to believe that last night had been anything but chance. For her to hide out in the yard was just so... childish.

She was about to get up and go back inside when a tree across the yard moved. A thrill of terror bored into her stomach and rooted her to the spot. Moments later, a large shape emerged from the tree line.

The thing was a blob, larger than a dog or any other creature she'd seen. It grunted as it shambled toward her hiding spot and huffed heavy breaths with the effort of its own weight. As it drew closer, the fear in her stomach grew and threatened to turn to panic. The dark blob was a bear.

It stopped, reared up on its hind paws, and sniffed the air. Then, it grunted.

From behind, more animals came from the tree line. Many of them appeared to be the same ones from the night before, but there were others that she either didn't see before or were newcomers.

She sat, terrified, unable and unwilling to move. What if they saw her? Were bears vicious? The thing's paws were the size of her head with claws like steak knives. If it chased her, could she get inside before it caught her? And what would she tell Grandma and Grandpa?

As her mind fought a battle to run or stay, another figure emerged from the tree line. Unlike the others, it wasn't dark as it approached. The white dress was unmistakable. It was the girl. On the ground, Hadley got a better look at her. The white dress was a simple thing with a lacy collar and sleeves. Her hair was done up in pigtails, and she wore no shoes. As she came closer, it became clear to Hadley that she didn't just bear a passing resemblance to Mom's missing sister, Patricia. She looked *exactly* like her, even down to the dress that the missing girl wore in one of the pictures in her mother's room.

The girl walked to the front of the group of animals and stopped in front of the bear. She took its massive head in her hands and buried her face in its fur. The beast groaned then shook its shaggy body. It looked as if she were whispering in the bear's ear.

The girl stiffened as if she'd heard something and then slowly turned her head. When her eyes met Hadley's, the liquid cold of dread spread throughout her midsection.

"Why, hello, Hadley." The little girl grinned.

Hadley clambered to her feet as her nerve lost its battle with her gut. That the girl knew her name was, for some reason, more unsettling than a full-grown bear standing less than twenty feet from her. She scrambled up onto the porch and darted back inside. The screen door gave a loud slap, but she didn't care. Nor did she care about the loud creaks the door's hinges seemed to just remember they were supposed to make. She locked the deadbolt and ran up the stairs as fast as she could go, ignoring the shrieking steps as she took the steps two at a time. By the time she got to her room, she was certain she'd awakened the whole house, but didn't much care.

She closed her bedroom door and leaned against it, panting as her heart pounded its way through her ribs. A moment passed without anyone banging on her door and demanding to know what was going on. Then another. A handful more and she let her breathing slow a bit. She crept to the French doors and sank down onto her hands and knees, then she crawled out onto the balcony.

Surely, they couldn't still be out there. They must have other, more important, things to do.

Hadley leaned up over the rail just enough so she could look down and see what was in the yard.

The little girl still stood, bone still, right below her window, staring up. Again, their eyes locked. The little girl smiled then turned and took her parade of animals back into the woods.

On the wind, Hadley could swear she heard the little girl's voice.

Come play with me, followed by a giggle.

CHAPTER FIVE

When morning came, Hadley saw its arrival. There were too many questions in her mind for sleep to come. And that the little girl knew her name filled her with such dread that she spent the rest of the night huddled against the headboard of her bed with a pillow clutched tightly in her lap. When the sun's first rays filtered through the windows, relief washed over her. She waited until Grandma's familiar stomps on the stairs came before she climbed out of bed and got dressed for the day, exhausted but no longer afraid. In fact, she felt exhilarated.

The little girl was real, that much was certain. She'd seen her up close. The animals too, so much so that she could smell the forest on the bear's fur.

By the time she got down the stairs, her brothers were already at the kitchen table. Grandpa sat in front of a big mug of coffee, morning paper open to the section marked "Politics." Grandma puttered by the stove cooking up scrambled eggs and bacon. A plate loaded down with toast already sat on the table, next to a glass carafe of maple syrup and a dish of what appeared to be hand-churned butter.

"Bout time," said Grandma as Hadley got to the last step. "I was beginning to think you were going to sleep the day away."

"No chance of that, eh sweetie?" Grandpa looked at her over the top of his newspaper and cocked an eyebrow. How did he know?

Hadley took a plate from the counter and held it while Grandma piled it high with eggs and bacon then split a biscuit and covered the halves with gravy. As she took her seat, she poured herself a glass of orange juice.

Whether she missed the city or not, she had to admit that Grandma's food was way better than anything she'd ever gotten from a fast food place in town. The eggs were fresh from Grandma's chickens, the orange juice came from orange trees on her property, and even the biscuits were scratch made. It amazed her how Grandma had the time and skill to cook the way she did and still keep up with the house and teach, but maybe there was a little magic in Grandma that didn't involve actual spell-work.

Between bites, she glanced at Grandpa. He kept reading his paper, though he occasionally did meet her eyes. Josh and Cole paid her no attention, as if the conversation from the previous day was completely forgotten.

"Grandma," she said, once she'd plucked up the nerve. "I saw the little girl again last night. In the yard. With all the animals."

"It was probably a dream," said Grandma with a dismissive wave. "Ain't no little girls 'cept you for miles around."

Something about the way she spoke, the way she kept her eyes on her plate, let Hadley know there was more that Grandma wasn't saying. Almost as if by saying the little girl wasn't real, she could will it to be true. She decided to let the issue drop without telling her that she'd gone outside and seen her up close.

"Probably just a dream," echoed Grandpa. "Best not to dwell on it. Wouldn't go chasing it, neither."

He peered at her over the top of the newspaper again. He knew. He absolutely knew she'd been downstairs and knew the little girl was real to boot. So why were they both being so evasive about it?

She ate the rest of her breakfast as Grandma talked about the lessons of the day. Illusionary magic, she called it, the way of making things seem like something they're not. As an example, Grandma passed her hand in front of Hadley's juice. One moment, it was the bright orange color of fresh juice. The next, it went clear and looked like water.

"Now, you know it ain't water, and I know it ain't water," she said. "But someone who didn't see me do that wouldn't know the difference. That's what it means to cast a glamour. It means to make something seem like what it ain't."

"But why would I want to do that?"

"Pranks!" said Cole.

"Fun!" said Josh.

"Lots of reasons," said Grandma with a withering look toward the boys. They just grinned. "But it's important for you to know how to do it so you'll know it when you see it. Understand?"

"I think so," she said.

"Could we use it to look like we're awake when we're asleep?" Cole bounced up and down in his chair.

"Or like our room is clean when it isn't?" Josh's eyes widened with the possibilities.

"This is why I ain't teaching this to you two yet," said Grandma. "You ain't old enough. You two'll use it for mischief! Now go on outside and play. And don't let me catch you starting no fires, neither."

"I'll keep an eye on them," said Grandpa with a chuckle as he followed them outside.

"Those boys are going to be a handful for your poor momma," said Grandma once they were gone.

It begged a question that hadn't occurred to her before.

"Why didn't Mom teach me about this stuff herself? Why'd she keep it a secret?"

Grandma was quiet for a moment, as if searching for the right way to phrase the answer.

"Your momma learned all of this when she was your age," she said. "She lost her spark over time."

"When Daddy died," said Hadley with a nod.

"No," said Grandma. "She lost her spark a long time before that. Just sort of lost her way. She got all caught up in the modern world, and I suppose she just forgot a lot of it. She still knows it, somewhere deep inside. And I reckon she still uses some of it, whether she realizes it or not. But I don't reckon she's confident enough to teach you. That's why she never told you."

"Then why'd she tell them?" she nodded toward her brothers. "They're not even old enough to practice."

"She didn't," chuckled Grandma. "They figured it out. You know as well as I do those boys know things they oughtn't. Anyways, she couldn't very well bring you here and leave them behind, now could she? If she didn't believe in herself enough to teach you, ain't no way she could deal with boys busting with magic like them. She just don't have it in her."

"Why not?" The answer was obvious, even though she couldn't say it out loud. The loss of her sister, Patricia, probably wrecked her confidence.

"Never you mind," said Grandma with a sad smile. "Let's just focus on what's what for now."

The lessons of the glamour were easier for Hadley than making fire. It took her only a couple of tries to disguise orange juice as water and to change the color of her t-shirt from white to blue. Grandma said that the principles behind both types of magic were the same, but she didn't see how they could be.

After lunch, Grandma again said that she and Grandpa had errands to run and asked that Hadley be the responsible one in the house. The boys looked ready to burst with mischievous energy, but Hadley figured she could handle them. Besides, she had other things she wanted to do and couldn't while under Grandma's watchful eye.

As the old truck made its way down the drive, the boys stood behind Hadley.

"It's against the rules," said Josh.

"You're not supposed to," said Cole.

"You two are creepy sometimes, you know that?"

They looked at each other and grinned, then they nodded.

"We know."

"Look," she said. "I'm just going to take a look. Can I trust you two to not do anything dangerous while I'm gone?"

They nodded but looked fearful.

Just like everything else, they already knew what she had planned. And just like every other time she broke a rule, they warned her against it. But they wouldn't tell. They never had in the past, anyway. She had no reason to believe they'd tell on her this time.

"Be careful," said Josh. "The woods aren't right. Just a little ways, then straight back, right?"

"Just keep an eye out," she said. "In case Grandma and Grandpa come back."

The boys nodded and then took a seat on the porch swing.

It wasn't a very complicated plan, and there wasn't any deviltry to it. She was just curious, and curiosity couldn't be a crime, could it?

From the edge of the porch, the tree line looked almost like a solid wall, a natural fence in the landscape. The view from the balcony showed it to be a neatly manicured circle around the house, but ground level revealed how massive the trees really were.

She lined herself up with her balcony and sighted the area where the little girl had come out, then walked a straight line toward the trees. When she came to the edge of the grass, she stopped.

"Be careful," shouted the boys in unison.

She waved back at them without looking. One more step and she would be past the tree line. One more step, and she'd break the rules again. Whatever was in the woods, Grandma didn't want her to know about it. And, for some reason, that scared her.

The woods aren't right? What did they mean by that? Maybe it was because they'd never been in the woods and had spent their lives in a planned neighborhood. Or maybe there was something more to it. Either way, as she approached the edge of the yard, her stomach tingled. They were right; she wasn't supposed to be there. But she had to know more about the girl. Who she was, at least. Maybe even where she went.

She took a breath, swallowed her nerves, and took the step through the tree line. Just a few steps, she told herself, then she'd go back. She'd keep the house in sight, then she'd be safe. If she kept the house in sight, she couldn't get lost, could she?

As she crossed the line, her skin tingled, as if she'd walked through a giant electric spider web. She ran her hands along her arms and looked down, expecting to see tiny threads. But there was nothing. Maybe she'd cross the line and the electric sparks she felt would burn her. Maybe the forest would swallow her whole.

Nothing happened.

The way Grandma told her to stay away from it, she half-expected to burst into flames or for lightning to strike, or for monsters to peek out from behind the rocks in the woods and lick their chops. But there was nothing but more trees, more dirt, more rocks.

"It's okay," she called back. "There's nothing out here."

Silence responded. The hairs on the back of her neck prickled as she realized that there were no sounds at all. Not just her brothers, but there were no birds calling, no crickets, not even wind. She slowly turned back toward the house.

The twins were no longer on the porch. In fact, the porch looked strange, darker and distorted.

But where could they have gone, and so quickly? She'd only turned her back for a moment. If they'd run off while she was supposed to be watching them, Mom would kill her. More, it would just prove her point that she needed a babysitter after all. And twelve-year-old girls didn't need babysitters.

"Josh? Cole?"

"Hadley!" Their voices came back distorted, hard to understand. "Where'd you go?"

She took a step back toward the porch. As her foot touched the ground, the boys were back, as if they'd never left.

"Where'd you go?" Cole stood and ran toward the tree line. "One second you were there, then you were just gone!"

"So were you," she said. "That was weird."

The boys looked at one another, then back to her, wordless.

"Don't move," she said.

The boys nodded in unison.

Keeping her eyes on the boys, she took a backward step toward the woods, then another. As she crossed the tree line, the boys vanished, obscured by a greenish haze that gave the whole yard an unreal look to it.

"You're gone again," said one of the boys. He sounded as if he were speaking through loose springs or into a spinning fan blade.

"I'm here," she said. It had to be magic, the kind designed to keep children in the yard. But she wasn't a child anymore, and baby gates were for babies.

"Come back," said one of the boys. "You're not supposed to go out there."

Hadley turned and looked into the woods. She knew the yard. It was safe. But the woods were unknown, exciting.

"I won't be long," she said. "Keep an eye out for Grandma and Grandpa."

There was no way of knowing if they did as she asked. They never answered, and the weird barrier around the house kept her from seeing them. Still, she trusted them. They were weird, but they usually did as she asked. Besides, the barrier around the house was just too exciting and strange for her to not want to explore it. Maybe the little girl would know how it worked, assuming Hadley could find her.

The boys couldn't see her, so it stood to reason in her mind that, until she crossed the strange barrier, she wouldn't have been able to see anything in the woods either. Maybe there was a trace of the girl, some clue left behind that she could find. She took a few steps, eyes on the ground, until she found the clue: a piece of cloth, a scarf maybe, lay tangled in a bush. Maybe it got snagged when she ran out of the clearing. Maybe she left it there on purpose, hoping for Hadley to come and find her. Either way, it was a real sign that she hadn't been dreaming.

Something in the woods moved, rustling under the brush. It didn't sound big, but she didn't want to take the chance. She snatched up the scarf and hurried back to the safety of the yard and marveled as the barrier between the woods and safety closed behind her.

Dinner that night was another hearty meal from Grandma's skillful hands. Hadley, however, wasn't hungry. The barrier beyond the tree line bothered her. Was it, as Grandma taught her, just a glamour, or was it something else? And why was it there? It didn't seem to keep anything out or in, so what was the purpose of it?

She picked at her food with her fork until the question in her brain just wouldn't be silent anymore and came spilling out of her mouth.

"Why can't we play in the woods?"

The table fell silent as everyone stopped mid-bite and stared at her.

"The woods is no place for children," she said. "All manner of things out there."

"But mom played there when she was a kid," said Hadley. "She told us about it. And you told us you used to play there as a kid too."

"True," said Grandma. "But if I knew then what I know now, I'd have never left the house. Y'see, not everything what looks beautiful has your best interest at heart. There're plants out there with the most lovely crimson leaves that have a poison on them that seeps through the skin. There're serpents deep in the wood that a single bite can nip you off away from Grandma forever and steal all your tomorrows."

Hadley rolled her eyes. The fairy tale bit might work with children, but not with her.

"But we know how to stay away from them," said Hadley. "It's easy. We stay away from red leaves and stay away from snakes."

"Them's not the worst of what's out there," said Grandma, her eyes sparkling. It was as if she'd wanted to tell the old stories for a long time but had no one to tell them to.

"Wolves?" Cole sat up straighter.

"Bears?" Josh grinned at his brother.

"Worse," said Grandma, her voice low and conspiratorial. "Things out there ain't no one seen in a hundred years. Not that have come back to tell about it. Them woods is full of spirits. Not all of them is ghosts, if you take my meaning."

Hadley looked to her brothers then back again and shook her head.

"Ghosts is easy," said Grandma. "Ghosts is just someone what died and lost their way. They're just the same as they was in life, only maybe a little more so. If a woman cried a lot before she died, she'd come back and cry all the time. If they was mean in life, they're meaner in death. Y'see what I'm saying?"

Hadley nodded.

"But then there's other things in the woods. Things that didn't never die because they was never alive to begin with. They just always was. Them trees out there, they got memories. They know who lived on the land and who treated it right. They know who come and go, who carved their names on their bark. If you're good to them, they protect you. If you ain't, what they got to lose by letting the bad things get you?"

"What kind of bad things?" The way Grandma talked, it was almost as if she believed in the stories, heart and soul. And maybe she did.

"Fairies," said Grandma. "Gnomes. Redcaps. Goblins. All manner of things."

"Those things aren't real," said Josh with a snicker.

"Maybe not," said Grandma. "But when I was growing up, I heard the tale of a family with a brand new baby. That baby got stolen by the creatures in the woods and got replaced by a changeling."

"There's no such thing," said Cole. "In ancient times, twins like us were accused of being changelings."

"Who's to say you're not?" Grandma cracked a smile, the tension in her story gone for good. "Little devils, you are. Be just about right if you two was up to no good."

"But what about—"

"It's late," said Grandma. "No more stories tonight. That's all they are, stories. Truth is, I don't want you in the woods because it's dangerous. Old mine shafts, old graveyards—"

"Graveyards?" Hadley' interests perked up.

"—and all other such stuff. Last thing I need is to try to haul one of you out of an abandoned well or some such thing. Your mother would never let me hear the end of it. G'on now. To bed with you."

They took their turns hugging and kissing Grandma, then they made their way up to their rooms.

"How old does she think we are?" Hadley was in the lead. She knew the boys wouldn't answer, but she mostly spoke to hear her own voice. "We're not babies. Fairies and goblins. I stopped believing in that kind of stuff when I was six."

Of course, she also stopped believing in magic when she was six, too. But Grandma showed her it was real. And if magic was real, it stood to reason that maybe the other legends of things in the woods were real too. Maybe there were fairies and goblins, monsters and ghosts. Maybe there were things that were worse.

More than ever, it made her want to know who the little girl was and what she was doing in the woods after dark. She sent the boys off to brush their teeth, then she closed the door to her room so she could plan without distraction.

Chapter Six

The house settled into its nightly rhythm of deep sleep and breaths, snores and murmurs. Unlike the previous night, she knew what to listen for. Her brothers' sounds, she knew. They both snored, almost in unison. When one breathed out, the other breathed in so they sounded like a broken accordion when they slept. It was the rest of the house to which she needed to listen so she could tell when she could sneak out without being caught.

The raspy noise came from across the hall. Cole and Josh were asleep. She lifted up on the door as she pushed it open so the hinges didn't squeak this time. Then, she made her way down the stairs through her carefully planned path. At the second floor, she paused and listened again.

The breeze outside pushed at the walls and windows and made the old house seem like it too was breathing the deep and heavy breaths of sleep. Just above the breaths was Grandma's light snore from downstairs. But she didn't hear Grandpa.

She took her special path down the stairs to the first floor, then darted toward the back door and out into the moonlight. Once the door closed behind her, she breathed just a little easier.

The previous night, she'd hidden behind the porch. But if she wanted to know who the little girl was, she'd have to talk to her. Which meant she'd have to come out of hiding. But that didn't mean she wanted to sit brazen on the porch waiting, daring the little girl to come out of the woods. She needed to hide, but only until she got near. Then she could come out and ask her questions.

She ducked down into her spot beside the porch and watched. Sure enough, after a few long moments, a stag appeared at the edge of the tree line. The bear was nowhere to be seen. Like the other nights, the processional of animals stepped out of the woods like they belonged in Grandma's yard. And at the end of the line was the curious girl dressed in white. Hadley waited until she was well clear of the tree line and all the way to the stag before she stood up from her hiding spot.

"Hello," she said.

The little girl jerked and her eyes flashed green, but then she calmed when she saw who'd just spoken to her.

"You came down," she said. "I was hoping you would. I wanted to meet you."

"Who are you?" She hadn't planned to start off so bluntly, but it was the first question on her mind, the only one that really mattered.

"My name's Patricia," said the girl in white. "I used to live in this house, I think."

Hadley's head reeled. It wasn't possible. Patricia was Mom's younger sister. If she were really Mom's sister, she'd be older too, wouldn't she? Unless she was a ghost. But she was standing right in front of her, as solid as the animals she walked with. And if it wasn't her, why did they share a name?

"Do you live nearby?"

"I live out there," said Patricia.

"Where are your parents?"

The word seemed to perplex her, as if the concept of a mother or father was alien.

"Don't you have a mom? A dad?"

"I did once," said Patricia. "I think. It was so long ago. It's hard to remember anymore."

"And the animals? How'd you do that? Why do they trust you?"

"They trust me because they're my friends," she said. As she said the phrase, Hadley's eyelids grew heavier, not with sleep, but because she liked the sound of Patricia's voice. She liked being around her. Patricia was nice. Patricia was her friend. "Why don't you come with me and I'll show you?"

The suggestion snapped her out of whatever spell held her.

"I'm not supposed to," she said.

"But you did anyway," said Patricia. "Didn't you? You weren't supposed to come out of the house after dark, and I'm pretty sure you're not supposed to talk to strangers either, are you?"

Hadley shook her head.

"Come on," said Patricia. "I've got so much to show you. Why don't you just come with me into the woods and I'll explain everything."

A light came on in the kitchen. Someone was awake.

"If they catch you out here, you'll get in trouble," said Patricia. She turned and darted into the tree line.

Hadley had only a moment to think. What would she tell them if she got caught? If they didn't see her, they wouldn't know she wasn't asleep upstairs in her room.

A shadow moved across the kitchen window toward the door. Whoever it was, they were coming outside. Fear of being caught made the decision for her.

Hadley sprinted for the tree line, toward the spot where Patricia had disappeared. She just hoped she was still there when she crossed through the glamour, and she hoped that whoever came through the door wouldn't see her hiding on the other side.

She broke through the tree line like a runner breaking a ribbon, then she stopped with her hands on her knees, panting. Patricia stood in front of her with an amused smile on her face.

"Wow," she said. "You can be pretty fast."

Hadley turned back toward the house. The back door opened and Grandpa emerged. He scanned the darkened yard once, twice, then a third time before he stopped.

"Stay away!" he yelled into the darkness. "We don't want you around here!" Then he turned and went back into the house. Hadley didn't let out her breath until the light in the kitchen window went out. He yelled like he knew someone was in the yard, like he knew *who* was in the yard.

"That was close," she said. "He almost caught us."

Patricia nodded.

"I'm impressed," she said. "I didn't think you'd do it."

"I didn't think I would, either." In truth, the thought of breaking more rules both terrified and thrilled Hadley. Grandma seemed so dead set that the woods were no good and that anyone that came around was not to be trusted.

But Patricia was just a girl, like she was. And it had been so long since she'd had anyone her own age, another girl, around. The rule was dumb and completely unfair. And, in her mind, unfair rules needed to be broken.

"Do you want to come and see?" Patricia waved an arm behind her to the darkened woods.

She did. She really did. But she also wanted to enjoy the woods as she explored them. She was too tired and still a little jumpy from Grandpa's appearance.

"I need to get back inside," said Hadley. "But can I come out tomorrow night? I didn't exactly plan past talking to you tonight."

Patricia's disappointed expression lightened.

"Tomorrow, then," she said. "I have so much to show you."

She turned and hurried down the path deeper into the woods. Hadley watched her for a moment then went back through the barrier and into the yard. For a moment, she stood and listened, certain that Grandpa would step out from behind a tree or off the porch and give her a good talking-to. But the yard was quiet, save for the chirping of cicadas and crickets in the moonlight.

Tomorrow.

There was a lot to do, but her stomach fluttered with plans to make, supplies to gather, and with figuring out how to get away with it all.

She made her way back across the yard and into the house. Before she closed the back door, she took one more look toward the tree line. Patricia had run off, but for some reason she could still feel her eyes on her, as if she watched from the shadows. It was almost as if she could feel her warm breath on her neck. She shook the feeling off and closed the door, then crept back up to her room and went to bed.

CHAPTER SEVEN

Hadley spent the next day alternating between anxiety and exhaustion. She gathered a few supplies for the night, some water bottles and candy, a few apples and marshmallows, and stuffed them into her backpack, which she hid under her bed. Then, she hurried down the stairs to do her daily magic lessons so Grandma wouldn't become suspicious.

Throughout the day, she kept a wary eye on Grandpa. If he had seen her, surely he would tell. And if he hadn't, maybe he went and checked her bed. If he had found her missing, wouldn't he have told Grandma? She'd have to be more careful tonight and stuff pillows under the comforter so no one would realize she was gone.

The day's lesson was on spells of protection. Grandma told her that some creatures couldn't cross a line of salt while others couldn't cross a line of red brick dust. Creatures of one sort couldn't even cross a threshold uninvited.

She didn't understand what difference the color of the brick made or what special magic a threshold had, but she wrote it down in her special book and nodded along.

"Some creatures," said Grandma, "can't cross running water. It's as if the current grabs their spirit and drags them away. But in these woods here, the main thing you have to watch out for is the fairy-folk. Ain't but one thing can stop them, and that's cold iron. It burns their skin, so they try to stay away from it. Here."

She pulled from her pocket an old key on a leather thong.

"Put this 'round your neck," she said. "Wear it always. That way, the fairy-folk can't lay a finger on you. Not a finger."

Hadley did as she was told and then lifted the key to get a better look at it. It was black with age and red in places with rust, like one of the old-fashioned keys that people used on old doors in movies. It was strange, but she liked it and tucked it into her shirt.

"Thanks," she said.

"Now pay attention," said Grandma. "There's all kinds of fairy-folk, just like there's all kinds of people. Some of them ain't nice, and some of them are. The trick is, you'll never know which one is which until it's too late, so it's best to not trust any of them."

"When will I ever see a fairy?" She laughed. "It's not like Austin has a lot of them."

"You'd be surprised," said Grandma. "Ever seen a ring of mushrooms? Out in a park or in your yard?"

Sure, she had. The boys liked to kick them over, but they always grew back. They always appeared after a particularly heavy rain.

"Those are fairy rings," she said. "That's where the fairies come to do business. If you find one with flowers in the middle, that's where they come to pay tribute to fairy royalty."

Hadley doubted it, but on some level she accepted it. If she were going to accept that magic was real, surely she *had* to accept the existence of fairies. And if they were real, what else was real, too?

"That's enough for today," said Grandma. Then, to Grandpa, "Take the boys outside for a few minutes."

When they were outside and out of earshot, Grandma turned to Hadley. "Let me show you something."

Grandma waved her hand over an area of the kitchen wall. One moment, it was wood paneling in the same butter-yellow color as the rest of the room. The next, the wood rippled and flowed like fabric, and it was as if someone had dropped a curtain from in front of a doorway.

"Those boys don't need to see this," she said. "Not yet. This is my library."

Hadley stepped into the room. It was more a large pantry than anything else, but instead of canned goods, every shelf on every wall was covered, floor to ceiling, with books. Most of them looked like journals that Grandma had filled herself. Others carried titles like *The Farmer's Almanac* and *Cunningham's Guide to Candle Magic*. One book in particular caught her eye.

"*Magical Creatures Great and Small*?"

Grandma nodded and she pulled the thick tome off the shelf.

"Lots of information in here," she said. "Chances are, you'll never see most of these. But the ones that live close by are marked." From the pages were dozens of frilly, brightly colored strips of paper.

"Thank you," said Hadley.

"There's rules here too," said Grandma. "One, don't let your brothers in here. Not yet. They're too young and they'd likely mark up the pages with crayons. Two, put everything back where you found it, or as close as you can get it. That's it."

"Can I take the books up to my room to read them?"

"Of course, you can," said Grandma with a smile. "Just make sure you bring them back when you're done. Now, step out and let me show you how to get in."

When Hadley was beyond the threshold, Grandma made a motion like throwing something upward. The illusion popped into place.

"To get in, you have to drop the veil," said Grandma. "Do the same motion I did, but backwards. That key around your neck is like your library card."

Hadley raised her arms, grasped at the imaginary curtain in front of the door, and threw it downward. The door appeared without a sound.

"Good," said Grandma. "Now put it back."

She did as she was told. It was easy for her, so long as she kept the image of the illusion as a heavy curtain in her head.

"Anything you want to ask me, go ahead," said Grandma. "But if you can't find me, or if I don't rightly know off the top of my head, you can likely find answers in here."

It was a gift the likes of which she'd never received before. She loved to read, loved fantasy. And her summer was turning into a fantasy novel, but for real. Grandma had given her the greatest gift, a library for her perusal. Even better, a library she didn't have to share with her brothers.

"Thank you," she said. "I can't wait to read through them."

She dropped the veil again and stepped inside to select a few titles. As she did, her questions from the previous night came back to her. Maybe it wasn't the right time to ask, but the questions itched in the back of her brain. For all the things Grandma was willing to tell her, there were still questions she wouldn't answer, and Hadley couldn't figure why.

Upstairs in her room, Hadley set two books on her bed. One was the guide to magical creatures. The other was one of Grandma's journals. She'd picked the oldest looking of them and pulled it out of curiosity.

She took the old journal, flopped onto the bed on her stomach, and examined the cover. Cracks decorated the cardboard, splits in the once colorful paper. The worn corners and edges told of countless times young fingers had opened the pages and read back through the old passages. The spine, a simple staple-and-tape line, showed even more signs of age with more splits covered by new masking tape to hold the pages together. She opened the cover.

In this book, I begin my journey, it said. *As above, so below. An it harm none, do as thou wilt. So mote it be.*

The words were adorned with a single five-pointed star, and below it was Grandma's name in flourished script. How old was she, Hadley wondered, when she'd opened the book for the first time, written her name, and started to learn magic? And who had she learned from? Her mother, she'd said, but Hadley had never met her great grandmother and couldn't help but wonder what she was like.

Between the first pages were pressed flowers, each with notes about what they were, where they grew, and their uses. Though the flowers were old, older than even her mother, they were still vibrant and beautifully colored. She lightly touched one of the pages, and a petal from one of the flowers fell to the bed.

It was all so fragile.

She gently closed the book and put it aside, intent that she would read the whole thing, but when she could do so without further damaging it. Not that she thought Grandma would be angry, but the book was a piece of Grandma's childhood, her history, and she didn't want to be responsible for destroying it.

The book on creatures of the woods seemed like it would hold her interest. She still wasn't sure she actually believed in such things, but they were fun to read about. Goblins, brownies, fairies, and sprites were all in the realm of possibility in the woods, as were hundreds more species. If she even encountered one of them, she'd be thrilled. She flipped the pages and looked at the sketches of each creature and wondered what it would be like to know them all.

Hadley...

The voice echoed from across a great distance, like a whisper that grew in strength as wind carried it through the trees. She was warm and comfortable, nestled in the downy comforter on her bed at Grandma's house, her book tucked beneath her like a paper pillow.

"Hadley!" The voice cut through her sluggish consciousness. "It's dinner time!"

Her eyes snapped open as she pushed herself upright. How long had she been asleep? For a moment, she was worried she had missed Patricia, but the sun hadn't yet disappeared below the horizon. She still had time. She looked toward the door of her room and found her brothers staring at her.

"You're supposed to knock," she said.

"We did," said Josh.

"Only you didn't answer," said Cole.

"Fine." Her tongue was still thick with sleep, and her eyes were a little blurry. "I'll be right down. Out." The boys turned and scampered down the stairs.

Hadley rubbed her eyes and stretched. She wasn't even aware she'd gone to sleep until the boys woke her up. The book still sat open, the page on an entry on a thing called a "changeling." They were creatures that could take any shape they chose, however they wanted to be perceived. The book said they could also seem to control the woods around them, the winds, the waters, everything, but it was all just like Grandma's glamour spell. It was nothing more than illusion. She wondered what such a creature would be like in real life as she closed the book and rolled down off her bed.

Night came far too slowly for Hadley's liking. She sat through dinner while her brothers prattled on in their sing-song way about the strange things they'd done that day. Grandma dutifully listened while Grandpa read his paper without touching his food.

He never seemed to touch his food. And yet, he was a large happy man. How he got to be so without eating was a mystery. But equally mysterious was how Grandma endured her brothers' endless tales of broken sticks and chasing imaginary animals through the barn.

After dinner, she sat and listened to more of Grandma's magical lessons. During the day, she showed spells and how to do practical things. But in the evenings, after dinner when she was tired, Grandma preferred to sit in her chair and talk more about the spiritual side of magic. Unlike the Christian faith, what they practiced had both a God and a Goddess, a boy and a girl. That was because, Grandma said, there were two sides to every coin. There was no day without night, no happy without sad, no good without bad. If we had nothing against which to measure, we'd forget how good things were. And what was more, the God and Goddess had sides to them as well that represented the three stages of life.

All of it swam by Hadley's mind in a blur. She understood what Grandma was saying, but she wasn't sure if she really "got" it. It was enough, though, that the concepts were there, and that she had at least a tenuous grasp of them.

After dark, when everyone had gone to bed, Hadley lay in her room and listened for the telltale signs that the house was asleep. First, the noise from her brothers' room settled into a steady rhythm of deep breaths and light snores, as opposed to the fidgety giggles that came while they were awake. Then, she crept out of her bed and crouched by the vent in the wall.

Days ago, she realized Grandma and Grandpa's voices came through the vent, as if their room was directly below hers. If she listened closely, she could tell when they were asleep. Grandpa didn't snore or even take heavy old-man breaths in his sleep, but Grandma's heavy rasp let her know the old woman was in deep dreamland.

Over the past couple of days, she took every opportunity she could to practice getting down the stairs without noise. As she closed the back door behind her, she fairly glowed with pride at not having made a single sound. Then, she sprung off the porch and took off across the moonlit yard at a dead run. As the trees loomed closer, something pulled at her, drew her forward, and spurred her to run faster for the veil beyond the tree line. As she approached it, she didn't slow, but sped up, closed her eyes, and launched herself through.

She came to a staggering halt as the veil closed behind her. It was just like it was during the day. On the yard side, everything was vivid, brightly colored, even at night. But on the other side, the world seemed darker somehow, a bit more gray. She looked back toward the house. No lights on in the distorted windows. She'd gotten away with it.

"I was starting to wonder if you were coming," said Patricia as she stepped out from behind a tree. "You really did it."

"I said I would," said Hadley. "And we're friends, right? Friends don't let friends down, right?"

"Right," said Patricia with a broad smile. "C'mon. There's so much to see." She looped her arm through Hadley's and nodded toward the woods with an exaggerated first step.

There was, as Patricia said, plenty to see, and she made a fine tour guide. Every tree they passed, Patricia knew the type and how long it had been there. At a ravine, they stopped so Patricia could point down the crevice to caves that, local legend had it, were occupied by gnomes and cave trolls. They both giggled at the notion, but Hadley got the idea that maybe Patricia believed the stories, if only a little.

"I'd better be getting back," said Hadley. "I don't want anyone to wake up and find me gone."

"Is that likely?"

"What?"

"Do people often wake up and go searching for you?"

The absurdity of the question struck her. Of course not. They were asleep and would likely remain that way until morning.

"Well... no."

"Well, come on then! What are you worried about?" She didn't wait for an answer before she turned and bounded into the shadows. Hadley hesitated for a moment then took off after her. Through the darkness, she caught glimpses of Patricia in shafts of moonlight that came through breaks in the canopy. After a bit, she lost track of where she was or even what direction she ran, so long as she kept Patricia in sight.

When she lost sight of her, Hadley stopped and turned. The house was nowhere to be seen. Neither was Patricia. She turned in place slowly as she tried to get her bearings and figure out where she was, but every tree looked the same in the dark. Every shadow was just like the next and could've been anything from a rock to a mountain lion.

"Patricia?" she called. "Patricia! I lost you!"

"I'm right here."

The voice startled her, and she turned so fast she almost fell down. Patricia stood an arm's length away, an amused smile on her face.

"I wouldn't leave you all alone in the dark, silly," she said. "As soon as I noticed you weren't behind me anymore, I came back."

"Where are we?"

"Almost there," said Patricia with a twinkle in her eye. "I promise, you'll like this."

"Just don't run off again, okay?"

"I promise," said Patricia. She slipped her hand into Hadley's and tugged. "We're friends, right? And friends don't let friends get lost."

Patricia led her through the trees until they came to a clearing where a river ran through in the darkness. She put a finger to her lips and crouched. Hadley did the same, then they waited.

Moments passed during which she wanted to ask questions. Who she was, what she wanted, did she know Grandma and Grandpa and, if so, why they wouldn't talk about her. What did she know about the curious veil that surrounded the house or about her mother's missing sister? But she didn't want to break the quiet spell of the river that glinted in the moonlight.

"There's magic in the woods," whispered Patricia.

"That's what my Grandma says," said Hadley. "She's teaching me about magic."

"Magic is everywhere," said Patricia. "Especially at night, if you know where to look."

Fireflies blinked in the darkness, pinpricks of light against the night. She'd never seen so many of them in one place, swarms of blinking yellow and green. For that matter, she'd never seen them so late at night. Fireflies were a twilight phenomenon. To see so many in the dead of night had to be some kind of magic at work.

As she watched their gentle dance in the air, other animals came to drink at the river. A pair of foxes and their kits, deer, even a few raccoons stood side by side at the river's edge. She didn't dare say a word for fear the spell be broken.

They lost track of time, neither willing to let the night end. The animals, the trees, the secret shadows and whispers of crickets thrilled her, gave her a sense even greater than when Grandma revealed she came from a family of witches. Not only was she special, not only did she have the power of magic, she had a friend. Hadley made her way back toward the house, happy.

At the edge of the veil around the house, Patricia stopped. Hadley turned to face her, but she stepped backward, away from the house.

"Sun'll be up soon," she said. "You don't want them to catch you out here in the woods. You'll get in trouble."

"I don't care," said Hadley. "I had fun. I'm so glad I met you. This place is so much more fun with a friend around."

She smiled.

"I'll come back," said Patricia. "Tomorrow, if you like."

"Yes!" Of course, she wanted her to come back. Magic was great and all, but with only her brothers to talk to, she felt a grade-A case of cabin fever coming on. But things were different now. Before, even with all the magic and wonderment, she still really just wanted to go home. But now that she had someone to share it with, she couldn't wait for nightfall so that she could see Patricia again.

CHAPTER EIGHT

The next day seemed exciting for Hadley. First thing in the morning, she did her magical lessons with Grandma. After lunch, she took a nap under the guise of reading in her room. That evening, she ate supper and listened while Grandma told her about the history of witchcraft in America and about the guiding principles that formed what she called "The Rede." That night, she waited again until the moon was high, until everyone else was asleep, then crept out of the house to the woods. Patricia stood waiting as she'd promised. Everything about her was the same as it had been every night she'd seen her—her hair in braids, the same white dress—as if she had no other clothes or knew no other way to fix her hair. Not that it mattered as Patricia took Hadley by the arm and led the way into the trees for high adventure.

"What is this place?"

Patricia had brought them further than they'd gone the night before, past the magical river, beyond the caves that they neither one dared go in. They'd gone until they reached a small stone wall that stood only about as high as Hadley's knees.

"This used to be the border between the properties," said Patricia. "A long time ago."

"A wall this short couldn't possibly keep anything out."

"I don't think it was meant to," said Patricia. "Just mark the space. This is mine, that's yours, that sort of thing. C'mon."

She stepped over the wall and Hadley followed, entranced by every new sight and sound. The birds sounded different on the other side of the veil, more alive, more immediate. The floor of the woods smelled richer, more earthy. Even the light seemed more determined to find its way through the canopy in the world away from Grandma's house.

"I'm showing you this because I trust you," said Patricia. "You're my friend, and I'm trusting you not to tell anyone this is out here."

Ahead, Patricia stopped beside an old wooden structure. It was too small to be a house but seemed shaped the same way, with a peaked roof and a door.

"A shed?"

"I think so," said Patricia.

"What's it doing so far out here?"

"I don't know," she said. "But no one else comes out here. Not ever. So it's mine now."

Patricia made her way around to the other side of the shed.

"Yours? What do you mean, yours?"

"I come out here sometimes," she said. "When I don't want to be at home. I like it better out here."

"Where's your home?"

Patricia was quiet for a moment, her eyes down.

"Not far," she said. "I don't like it there. It's lonely."

She lifted a wooden plank that held the door shut, then gave the door a tug. With some effort, it creaked open.

"Come in," said Patricia. "This place is yours now, too."

It was warm in the shed, but not so much as she'd expected. The damp air smelled of rotting leaves and of mildew. No light came through the open door, as if it didn't want to intrude on the space. A moment later, the scent of sulfur hit her nostrils as Patricia struck a match and lit a small candle.

"I come here a lot," she said. "I find lost things and bring them here."

The dirt floor was covered in a tarp. On top of it, Patricia sat on a blanket. Around the tiny room were innumerable curious items. In one corner was a small collection of dolls, some broken, others dirty, that she'd no doubt found while walking through the woods. In the opposite corner were the bones of small animals, skulls and vertebrae.

"I didn't kill them, if that's what you're thinking," she said. "I found them. They seemed lonely, like me. So I brought them back so we could keep each other company."

It seemed strange to Hadley that a skull would seem lonely, but the more she thought of it, the more perfect sense it made. No more eyes to see, no more ears to hear, of course a skull would be lonely.

"Where'd you get the rest of this?" She moved along the walls and laid gentle fingers on jewelry, toys, forks and spoons, all exotic treasures in Patricia's collection.

"I found it all," she said. "Playing in the woods. I find lots of stuff."

"But how?" It didn't make sense. "No one comes in these woods, do they?"

"That doesn't mean they never did," said Patricia. "Some of this is really old. Some of it is from before I was born."

"What are you going to do with it all?"

"I don't know," said Patricia. "I've never had anyone to share it with before."

"Don't you have any brothers or sisters?" The question just jumped out of her mouth before she could pull it back. She looked just like the little girl in the pictures in Mom's room, the one that died. But that was impossible. She couldn't be the same Patricia that was Mom's sister.

"No," said Patricia quietly. "I had a sister once. She used to do things with me. But then one day, she just stopped."

The fine hairs on her arms prickled.

"I'm sorry," said Hadley. "I have two brothers. Josh and Cole. They're twins."

"Are they learning magic too?"

"They're not old enough," said Hadley. "They can already do some stuff, but they're still too young. Grandma says she'll teach them in a few more years, but for now, I'm the only one who gets to learn. They've figured out some stuff on their own."

"Like what?"

"They can start fires," said Hadley with a huff. "For them, it comes easy. It takes me more practice."

"What's it like, having twins for brothers? Do they do all the same things and finish each other's sentences and stuff?"

"They do," said Hadley. "They're kind of spooky sometimes. Most of the time they leave me alone, though."

"I don't like being alone," said Patricia. "I always wanted to have my sister back. Or maybe another sister."

"How about me?" The bitter loneliness in Patricia's voice made her say it. "We could be summer sisters."

Patricia looked up into her eyes in shock. For a moment, disbelief hung on her face, then split into a wide grin as she gave a vigorous nod.

"I'd really like that," she said. "I haven't had anyone to talk to in such a long time."

"Me neither," said Hadley. "And I really like spending time with you."

They shared an awkward hug, then settled back onto the blanket.

"I've never met twins before. Do you think maybe I could meet your brothers?"

"Summer sisters," said Hadley. "They're your brothers too, now. I think it's time you met."

Grandma told her not to let anyone into the house. About that rule, she was crystal clear. Strangers weren't welcome. But Patricia wasn't a stranger anymore. They were sisters, or as close as they could get for the summer anyway. And sisters were family, and as such, she should be allowed in.

"You can meet my Grandma and Grandpa too," said Hadley. "I know they'll love you."

Patricia grew silent and her smile vanished.

"I don't think I'm ready for that yet," she said. "Your grandpa came out and yelled at me, remember? He said I wasn't welcome. And I don't think your grandma will like me, either."

"I'm sure she would," said Hadley. "But if you'd rather, we can wait. Come tomorrow during the day. Grandma said she had to go back into town for a while. You can meet the twins then."

Patricia's face brightened a little and she nodded.

The walk back to the house was quiet, marked only by the chirping of crickets and the crunch of dead leaves beneath their feet. At the edge of the veil, Hadley turned back to Patricia.

"Tomorrow," she said. "I'll make sure Grandma and Grandpa are gone, then I'll come out to get you."

Patricia nodded, hugged her again, then darted back into the woods. Hadley waited until she could no longer see her white dress and then turned back toward the house. It was still dark, with hours before dawn broke, but she couldn't help but feel a little afraid. If she were caught, not only in the woods but after dark as well, what would Grandma and Grandpa say? Would they tell her mother?

Crossing the veil felt like wrapping herself in film, like everything inside the yard was made to hold her in, to bind her and keep her from experiencing anything. When she left the yard, she felt free, like she'd just shed a second skin. But the return always made her feel trapped. She scanned the house for movement or lights, found none, then sprinted across the yard. She was relieved to find the back door as she'd left it, unlocked, and hurried up the stairs to her room.

"Where were you?"

Her stomach lurched at the voice. She'd been caught, she knew it, and all her plans were over. But a moment later, her bedside lamp clicked on revealing Cole and Josh on her bed.

"Don't do that," she whispered. "You scared the crap out of me."

"Don't say crap," said Cole.

"Well, you just did," she replied. It was an old game. She often said worse and worse things just to see what she could get them to say, but she wasn't in the mood.

"Where were you?" Josh locked eyes with her, ignoring his brother.

"I was in the woods," said Hadley. "With my friend."

"You're not supposed to be in the woods," said Cole.

"You won't tell, will you?"

The twins looked at each other, then back to her, and shook their heads.

"Good," she said. "The girl I met, her name's Patricia. She lives in the woods. She's close to my age."

"She's a stranger," they said together.

"No," said Hadley. "Look, I don't have anyone to talk to. Mom took me away from all my friends, and I had a really fun summer planned and... It just wasn't fair. I didn't want to come here in the first place."

"Neither did we," said Josh. "But you're learning magic—"

"And magic is great," she said. "And I'm having fun with it, and it's really cool. But I don't have anyone to talk to. You at least have each other. You two are more than brothers. You're best friends, too. I don't have anyone like that. At least I didn't. Then I met Patricia."

"What is she doing in the woods?" Cole glanced to his brother, then back again. "Where does she live?"

"She's a neighbor," said Hadley. "She lives out past the woods. But we've been going hiking. She's been showing me the area. I love it out there. She wants to meet you."

The boys shared a wary glance.

"I don't think that's a good idea," said Josh. "Maybe we should ask Grandma—"

"No!" said Hadley. "I'm the oldest, and that means what I say goes, and I say we're not asking Grandma! Look, she's afraid Grandma and Grandpa won't like her. I told her she could meet you both. Please?"

The twins looked at each other again without saying a word. For a long moment, they stared intently at each other, then they turned back to Hadley and nodded.

"Thank you," she said. "She's coming tomorrow while Grandma and Grandpa are in town."

"Grandpa?" Cole looked at her quizzically.

"Didn't you notice? Whenever she leaves, he's riding with her. They never go anywhere without each other. Now go to bed."

They did as they were told and closed her door softly as they left. When they were gone, she lay back on her pillow and smiled.

Morning came, and despite her limited amount of sleep, Hadley awoke happy. Not only did she have a friend, but a summer sister. Her brothers would meet Patricia, and together they would convince Grandma and Grandpa to let her come to the house. Then, summer wouldn't seem so long, so lonely. And maybe Grandma could teach Patricia magic, too. Then maybe she could find out why she looked so much like Mom's sister.

She ate breakfast quickly, washed and put away her dishes, then hurried back upstairs to shower and dress. By the time she was done, Grandma was already gathering her keys and her purse.

"I won't be long," she said. "Just got a few errands. You sure you don't want to go with me today?"

"No, thanks," said Hadley. "I'm practicing glamours. I think today I'll change my hair color to blue."

"Okay," said Grandma. "Stay out of trouble."

Hadley watched as Grandma got into her car. True to form, Grandpa sat in the passenger seat. When he noticed her, he waved and smiled, then the car lurched into gear and headed down the long gravel road that served as the driveway.

Once the taillights were gone, Hadley ran downstairs. The twins were waiting by the door.

"Are you sure about this?" Cole held his brother's hand, a thing he only did when he was afraid.

"Yes," said Hadley. "You'll see. Patricia's nice."

"Grandma said not to let strangers into the house," said Josh.

"She's not a stranger," said Hadley. "She's my friend. She's more than my friend. We're summer sisters. That makes her your sister, too."

The boys looked at one another, uncertainty etched on their faces.

"It'll be fine," she said as she went to the door, slipped her shoes on, and went out into the yard.

The yard was silent. Every other day, birds chirped or cicadas buzzed. But the wind was still, the air quiet. There wasn't even a whisper through the branches of the trees beyond the veil. She thought it odd but paid it no mind as she hurried to the tree line.

"Patricia," she called. "Are you there?"

The girl in white, always in white, stepped through the veil and faded into the tree line. She smiled and hugged her summer sister.

"Can I come in?"

"Yes," said Hadley. "But only for a little while. Grandma and Grandpa will be back soon."

"Do I get to meet your brothers?"

Hadley pointed to the porch where Josh and Cole stood, hand in hand. For a moment, Patricia seemed too excited to speak, then she slowly approached as if she were afraid of spooking them.

"Hello," she said. "I'm Patricia. You must be Josh and Cole."

The boys nodded.

"You're twins," she marveled. "I've never met twins before. Can you... I don't know... Read each other's thoughts or something?"

The boys said nothing, only continued staring at her.

"They do it all the time," said Hadley. "They hold whole conversations without speaking a word. They know things they shouldn't be able to know, too."

"Is that true? Do you see things no one else can either?" She smiled. For a moment, it seemed to Hadley that the twins shared a shudder, but she dismissed it as the boys being nervous to meet new people, as they often were.

"It's a beautiful house," said Patricia. "I'd love to see the inside."

The boys shot a look of panic to Hadley, but she rolled her eyes and dismissed it.

"Sure," she said. "Come on in. You're family, remember?"

Hadley opened the door and gestured toward the inside. Patricia stood on the porch and stared, as if she were afraid of whatever lay inside. The smile she wore in the yard faded until her face wore a blank expression, neither playful nor serious. She looked from corner to corner, from ceiling to floor, and took tentative steps into the living room. For a moment, her wide eyes and placid face made Hadley uneasy.

"It's so beautiful," said Patricia after a few moments. "Just like I knew it would be."

She crept from room to room on the bottom floor, slowly dragging her fingers across shelves, across the couch, across the kitchen table. Nothing looked particularly beautiful to Hadley. Everything was just normal, everyday stuff to her. But Patricia seemed to find everything just one step short of royalty.

In the kitchen, she stood in the doorway and stared at the table where they ate. Then, she slowly crossed the room and took a seat. Hadley's own, in fact.

"That's where I sit," said Hadley. "During mealtimes."

"Must be nice," said Patricia. Her voice had a dreamy quality to it, like she was lost in memory.

Patricia stood and walked around the edge of the kitchen. At the veil in front of Grandma's library, she paused, looked the wall up and down, then continued on her way.

She paused at the fireplace mantle where pictures stood in frames and stared at each one as if memorizing the faces.

"Who are they all?"

"Some of them are Grandma and Grandpa," said Hadley. "Most of them are of my mother. Some are relatives I haven't even met."

Patricia took down a photograph and stared deeply into it.

"Who's this?"

"That's my mom," said Hadley. "She lived here as a kid. She's on a business trip right now. That's why we're staying with Grandma and Grandpa."

"Your mother was an only child?"

"No," said Hadley. "She had a sister who died."

"And why are there no pictures of her?"

It struck her as odd, but then as a very good question. Why *were* there no photographs of Mom's Patricia? And why did her Patricia sound almost bitter with the question?

She put the photo back in its spot and then drifted through the room toward the stairs.

"Is your room up here?"

"Two floors up," said Hadley. "The whole second floor is locked up."

Patricia looked upward and climbed with Hadley close behind. There couldn't be any harm in going up to look. After all, the rooms were locked, and she'd already broken the rules by letting her in. She couldn't possibly get into more trouble.

When she came to the second floor, Patricia moved to the center of the room of doors and turned in place, looking from one to the next.

"They're all locked?" She moved to the first door and put her hand on it.

"Yes," said Hadley. "Grandma doesn't want anyone in those rooms."

"Why not?" Patricia pushed lightly on the door. "What's in them?"

"Memories," said Hadley. "That's what Grandma says. Although, I did go into one of them that was unlocked."

"You went into one?" Cole's voice startled her. She hadn't heard them following up the stairs.

"It was just Mom's old bedroom," said Hadley. "From when she was a kid. Anyway, the door wasn't locked at first. It is now, though."

"Did you take anything from the room?" Patricia's voice sounded far away, like she wasn't even aware of asking the question.

"A book," said Hadley. "A diary. I tried to put it back, but someone had already locked the door. I'll have to find a way to put it back before I leave."

Patricia drifted toward the last door in the row and stopped in front of it.

"I wish I could go inside one of them."

"That one was my mom's. That's the one I went in."

She nodded then slowly walked to the second door.

"I want to see what's in this room," she said. "This one in particular."

"Why?"

"I don't know," she said. "I just think this room would be interesting."

The way she spoke, the sound of her voice, made Hadley uneasy, like maybe she'd made a mistake in letting her in. But that couldn't be right. They'd shared secrets, talked about private things. Patricia even showed her the private collection in the woods. Patricia trusted her, which meant Hadley could trust Patricia.

"Come on," she said. "Up one more flight. That's where my room is. It's the best room in the house."

"Is that where your room is, too?" Patricia turned her gaze toward the twins. They neither nodded nor said anything.

"Yes," said Hadley. "Both rooms are up here. But mine's nicer. Come see."

Patricia stared at the door for a few moments more before Hadley took her by the hand and gave her a gentle tug.

It seemed to do the trick, as she snapped out of whatever spell the door held and followed her up the stairs.

At the top, she stopped again and looked around.

"It's a big space," she said. "Which room is yours?"

Hadley pointed to the closed door at the end of the hallway, then turned to see the twins in the doorway to their room.

"They're both in there?"

"They never go anywhere without each other," said Hadley. "I mean, it's weird, but it also makes them easy to find. Wherever you find one, the other one is right there, too."

Patricia nodded and then walked down the hallway toward Hadley's door.

"May I?"

"You are welcome," said Hadley with an over-exaggerated bow. "Enter, my summer sister."

Patricia giggled at the false pomposity, then curtsied and opened the door. By her reaction, Hadley guessed the room far exceeded whatever she'd expected.

"It's huge!" she said as she turned in circles. "It's like a whole other house all to yourself!"

"It's got its own bathroom too," said Hadley. "I don't have to share the one in the hall with my brothers."

"And this bed, it's all yours?"

"Yep," said Hadley. "Just me."

"But it's so big! A whole family could sleep in it!"

"I know," said Hadley. It dawned on her that Patricia's reactions indicated she'd never seen such luxury, and she'd never really answered before. "Where do you live?"

Patricia grew still and quiet, made a good show of being interested in something on the dresser.

"Through the woods," she said. "Not too far."

"Maybe I could visit your house," said Hadley.

"I don't know," said Patricia. "My family... They don't like strangers either, and they're always around."

Hadley thought for a moment. She recognized a person ashamed of their home, and the last thing she wanted to do was rub her privilege in her friend's face. She also didn't want to push the issue, embarrass her further.

"Well, we'll just hang out here," she said after a moment. "Or at your place in the woods. Either way. You're welcome here."

"Are you sure?" Her voice took the dreamy quality again. "That I'm welcome, I mean? Your grandparents might not like me."

"Grandma told me to consider this my room," said Hadley. "And since it's mine, I can have whoever I like in it. And you're family now, and family is always welcome. So I say you are always welcome in my room."

Patricia turned and smiled at her, and honest genuine look of pleasure.

"Thank you," she said.

"Come on," said Hadley. "I have to show you the balcony, where I read."

"Is that where I saw you before?"

To answer, Hadley grabbed her hand and took her to the French doors and opened them wide.

"I can see the whole yard from here," she said. "It's the best view in the house."

"I love it," said Patricia.

They stood for a moment and enjoyed the summer air, then the stillness was interrupted by a soft whine from far away.

"That'll be Grandma's car," said Hadley. "They'll be here soon."

"Oh, no!" Patricia hurried inside and ran toward the bedroom door. "I can't let them find me here. I don't want to get you in trouble."

Before Hadley could stop her, Patricia ran out the bedroom door, her steps on the stairs impossibly loud and fast, and then to the second set before Hadley even made it to the bedroom door. She ran back to the balcony in time to see Patricia dart across the lawn. At the tree line, she turned and waved, then disappeared beyond the veil as Grandma and Grandpa's car came trundling up the driveway. The car came to a stop and they got out, giving no indication they'd seen the strange girl in white run across their lawn.

It was ridiculous that her friend couldn't stay. She'd talk to them as soon as they were inside and make them understand that Patricia was important to her. Then they'd have to let her maybe spend the night, or even stay the week. Lessons were better with a study buddy.

She made to leave her room, only to be stopped by the twins who stood in her doorway.

"You shouldn't have brought her here," said Cole.

"Grandma said no strangers," said Josh.

"She's not a stranger," said Hadley. "She's—"

"She's bad," said Cole with enough emphasis to startle her. "You shouldn't have invited her in."

"She is *not*," said Hadley. "You're being stupid. You both are. You two have each other and I don't have anyone. I find someone and you tell me she's bad? *You're* bad. If you don't like her, then stay away from us both."

She turned and went back in her room, all thoughts of telling Grandma and Grandpa about Patricia gone, and slammed the door in her brothers' stupid faces.

Chapter Nine

H adley spent the rest of the day in her room, unwilling to talk to or see anyone. She sat cross-legged on her little balcony, a tiny piece of tinder smoldering in front of her. The angrier she got, the more the little wooden piece glowed red.

The boys were being stupid. They didn't even know Patricia, just immediately decided she was bad. It wasn't right. Patricia acted strange, but it didn't mean anything. She was in a new place with things she'd never seen before. Patricia's family was probably poor and she thought Grandma and Grandpa's house to be more a castle than a farmhouse. It was little wonder she seemed odd.

By the time lunch came about, she was certain Josh and Cole would tell Grandma and Grandpa about Patricia. It would be just like them to spoil it by telling first, not letting her explain herself. She came down the stairs into the kitchen to find both grandparents and her brothers already seated at the table. She took her seat and ate her lunch, a grilled cheese that Grandma had cooked perfectly, with a glass of scratch-made lemonade. The conversation was light, friendly even, without even a mention of strangers or girls in the woods. After a few minutes, it became clear the boys hadn't told. They sat on the opposite side of the table casting accusing glares at her between bites, but they didn't volunteer any information.

When lunch was finished, she helped wash the dishes and put them away. As she dried, she tried to come up with some way to bring up the subject of Patricia without it seeming awkward and without admitting that she'd already invited her into the house.

"Grandma," she said. "Aren't there any other people my age around for me to hang out with?"

"Oh, no, dear," said Grandma. "I'm sorry. If you like, I can take you to the mall later. But I'm afraid it's just us for miles around."

"What if there were someone?" She didn't make eye contact. "Would it be okay to have them over?"

Grandma put down the frying pan she'd been washing and eyed Hadley closely.

"You haven't been in the woods, have you? I done told you, stay out of the woods. You seen someone in the woods? Have you?"

"No, Grandma," she lied. "I just wanted to know."

"Don't never bring nobody into this house, and don't go out into them woods. Y'hear me? You see someone creeping around in them woods, you let me know. I put that veil around this house for a reason."

"It *was* you who put it up!"

"Well, of course it was me," said Grandma. "Who else'd you think it would be? Santa Claus?"

"But why? Things come in and out of the veil all the time. What's the point of it?"

"Never you mind," said Grandma. "It's kept bad things out for years. If bad things are coming through it now, I gotta fix it."

"But..."

"You mind me, missy! Don't you go letting nobody into this house!"

"Yes, Grandma," said Hadley.

She made her way back up to her room. Every step on the old stairs creaked in a way that made it seem that the house itself was lonely. She took them slow as she tried to think of another way to get Grandma to let her bring her friend over. Surely, Grandma didn't know *everyone* in the woods. If she did, she'd have known Patricia was a nice person. Maybe she just didn't realize Patricia lived nearby. Except, Patricia told her she'd lived there for a long while, and the shed in the woods was full of things she'd collected, things that had taken years to accumulate.

Most likely, Grandma didn't know her neighbors at all. They lived so far away, after all, and she never had any visitors.

This was all Mom's fault. Her fault for her stupid business trip. Her fault for not teaching her about magic herself. Her fault for leaving Hadley and the boys out in the middle of the wooded nowhere. Her fault for Daddy.

The thought took her by surprise, how much she missed him. She'd thought she was over it, the grief, the loss. It would've been easier if Daddy had left or divorced Mom. It would've been easier if Mom had cheated on him or been cruel to him. But she sent him out. She sent him to the grocery for something stupid and selfish.

It was ice cream. It was one specific flavor of ice cream, one only made one time of year in Texas, and whenever it came out Mom just had to have it. 1908 Vanilla, that was the flavor. And it was good, all right. But Mom had a craving, and Dad never told her no.

When the police got to the house, Mom was already worried. Hadley sat on the stairs wondering why Mommy cried. Josh and Cole stood next to her, their expressions blank.

"Daddy's dead," they said. She didn't ask how they knew, but she believed them.

Mommy cried, screamed, and begged the police officers to tell her it wasn't true, that it was a joke, that she wouldn't be mad if they just came clean. The poor officers stood with their hands in their pockets with rehearsed lines of condolences and then turned and left. Mommy sank to the floor and wept, but it didn't do any good. Daddy was gone. He wasn't coming home. All because Mommy wanted ice cream.

Hadley hadn't been able to touch the stuff since. Chocolate, strawberry, especially vanilla, made a lump come up in her throat and brought tears to sting her eyes.

She rounded the next flight of stairs. Patricia would be disappointed. She really wanted to come and meet the family, now more than ever since she'd seen the inside of the house. How would she explain to her friend that Grandma just wouldn't listen?

She came through the door to her room and closed the door behind her.

"Well?"

The voice came from out on the balcony. She spun and looked to see Patricia behind the curtains on the French doors.

"How did you get up here?" Hadley hurried to the doors and opened them.

"I climbed, silly," said Patricia, though she didn't smile. "What did your Grandma say?"

"I tried," said Hadley. "Really, I tried. She just wouldn't listen. I'm going to try again, though. Later. Maybe tomorrow."

"I see," said Patricia, her voice frosty. "I thought we were friends. Summer sisters."

"We are," said Hadley. "Just give me some more time. I'll—"

"I have to go," said Patricia. "But don't worry. I'll still be around."

Before Hadley could stop her, Patricia dropped over the side of the balcony. For a moment, she thought for sure her friend would fall and break a leg or worse. She raced to the side and found Patricia halfway down the wall, climbing with skill she wouldn't have guessed for a girl in a white dress. When she reached the ground, she turned back and looked up at Hadley without smiling, then darted off into the tree line.

Hadley stared after her for a moment and then turned to go back downstairs. Grandma needed to give her an answer. She might not be old enough to drive yet, but she was old enough to learn magic, which meant she was old enough to walk in the woods if she wanted to. Grandma's rules were silly and outdated. If someone like Patricia could roam the woods without so much as getting her pretty white dress dirty, surely it was safe enough.

Halfway down the stairs, Grandma's voice met her. It was half a conversation, which told her she was on the phone. Likely with Mom.

"I don't know," she said. "I think maybe she went into the woods. Of course, I told her not to. Did that ever stop you? She don't know what's out there. She wouldn't believe me any more than you did. Well, I don't want her to find out the same way. Your sister—yes."

Wait. What?

"Yes. I'm sorry. They'll be safe as long as they stay with me or inside the tree line. Even if it can get past the veil, the house is safe. Won't be nothing that can get in unless she done something really stupid. Then we're all in trouble."

Stupid, like maybe breaking all of Grandma's rules?

"Alright. I'll call. I said I would. I love you too, sweetie. Bye."

Whatever she and Mom were talking about, it involved her, and she figured she needed know about it. She hurried down the stairs and found Grandma at the kitchen table with a satellite phone in her hand.

"So phones do work out here," said Hadley.

"Just this one," said Grandma. She still seemed cheery, but there was a hint of sadness to her voice. "You heard?"

"Some of it," she said. "That was Mom, wasn't it?"

Grandma nodded.

"Why can't I go out into the woods?"

"There's all sorts of critters out there," said Grandma. "You're better off staying here."

"Why? What's out there?"

"Oh," said Grandma. "Bears, bobcats, coyotes. Lots of things. Things that like to eat children that get too close to 'em."

"I've been in the woods," said Hadley. "I didn't see any animals like that."

The old woman's speed was surprising, frightening even, as she leapt from her chair and closed the distance between them.

"What did you see? You tell Grandma, eh? What did you see?"

"Nothing," she stammered. "Nothing. I went through the veil into the woods, but..."

"You was asking about bringing someone over." Grandma narrowed her eyes. "Did you meet someone out there in the woods? You tell me. You tell me true, now, y'hear?"

Whether it was the intensity of Grandma's stare or the fury in her voice, she couldn't bring herself to tell her about Patricia. She wouldn't understand.

"No," she said. "Just wishful thinking. I'm just so lonely out here."

"Stay out of the woods," said Grandma. "No more. Your ma will be back just a couple of days. You can go home and you can do your magic learning from her. Until then, just stay out of the woods. Y'hear me?"

"Yes, ma'am," said Hadley.

Grandma's grip on her arms softened, and the fire in her eyes faded to the kindness she recognized. Grandma nodded, and Hadley ran back up the stairs. At the top of the first flight, she rounded the corner and found Josh and Cole at the top of the second flight.

"You lied," said Josh.

"You shouldn't have lied," said Cole.

"She wouldn't have understood," said Hadley. "Besides, what does it matter? Patricia's mad at me, and I don't think she's coming back."

"I hope not," said Josh.

"You guys are the worst." Hadley finished climbing the stairs and went into her room and slammed the door. "I hate it here."

The rest of the day, Hadley spent in her room. She didn't read, didn't practice magic, didn't look out the window, just lay on her back in her bed, staring at the ceiling and trying to make sense of the one-sided phone call she caught. If Mom didn't think they were safe, why'd she drop them off here in the first place? Grandma knew all about the veil. It seemed obvious that Grandma put it there. But why, she couldn't even begin to guess. Deer and squirrels came through it just fine, so it couldn't be there to keep the forest animals out. Patricia even came through with ease.

More important, what exactly was it? Was it like the one that kept the boys from seeing the library?

Grandma talked about the animals of the woods. "Critters," she called them. But for as long as she'd been tromping the woods with Patricia, they never saw any sign of anything dangerous. In fact, the only thing she saw in the woods was her friend and the creatures that accompanied her. So what could Grandma be talking about?

She glanced out the French doors. Pinpricks of light shone in the velveteen sky. When had it gotten dark? And why had Grandma not called her for dinner?

Through the open doors, a peculiar sound came. At first, she thought it was a night bird, but then the song took rhythm, cadence, and she realized what she heard was a voice. A girl's voice. There were no words, only tones that drew her to the balcony and made her look down.

At the edge of the tree line, two familiar figures stood. They swayed like tall grass in the wind and then looked at each other. The song pulled them closer to the woods.

"Josh! Cole! What're you doing?"

They didn't seem to hear her but stepped through the tree line and into the woods.

"No!" she shouted and ran out the door to her room, down the stairs, and out to the lawn. The boys were nowhere to be seen. The song was gone. All that was left was the eerie silence of the night.

"Grandma! Grandpa!" She hurried into the house. Trouble or no, she had to come clean, had to get help to go and find her brothers. And if there were consequences, she'd gladly face them to get her brothers back.

"What is it, dear?" Grandma came out of her bedroom in a bathrobe, her long hair braided down her back.

"They're gone," she said. "You said not to go into the woods, but I did, and now they're gone."

"Who?"

"Cole and Josh," said Hadley. "I saw them out my window. They went into the woods."

"Oh, no," said Grandma. She shuffled Hadley aside and hurried out the back door to the lawn. "You boys! You come back now, y'hear? Get back here before I have to give your butts a good tanning!"

Silence came back from the woods, without even birds or insects to make a single noise. Grandma backed toward the house, then turned and ran back through the door and locked it behind her.

"Those boys," she said. "Why would they go out like that? You went into the woods? Even after I told you not to?"

From upstairs came a sound, so light and faint Hadley wasn't even sure she heard it. For a moment, she froze—until she figured out what the sound was. A giggle, high pitched and full of mischief. Patricia.

"You met one, didn't you?" There was no anger in her voice, no hint that Hadley would be in trouble. Just weary sadness. "You made a friend out there in the woods, didn't you?"

Hadley nodded. Her grandmother was as she'd never seen her. Before, when she reacted, Grandma was full of fear disguised as anger. This was different, stronger. There was fury in her spine, but beyond that Hadley saw an iron will that she'd have never before thought Grandma capable of.

"You invited it in," said Grandma. "Oh, by the old gods, you invited it in, didn't you?"

"Yes, ma'am," said Hadley. Her heart pounded in her chest and the acrid taste of fear soaked her tongue. Fingers tingled with the notion that something had to be done, if anyone could just figure out what.

Footsteps echoed through the house as small feet dashed across the landing on the top floor. Doors slammed while Grandma stared at the ceiling.

"It's Patricia," said Hadley. "She's playing a game, I think."

"It's a game, alright," said Grandma. "Not the one you think, but it's a game."

"Patricia! Come out!"

More giggles from upstairs.

"Go to my room," whispered Grandma, her eyes never leaving the stairwell. "In my bedside table. Get my book."

"Which one?"

"You'll know," she said, then she spoke louder. "You're not welcome here. You can't stay."

"I'll always be welcome," said Patricia in a voice that seemed to come from everywhere. "I'm family now, isn't that right?"

"The book. Now. Go!"

Hadley pulled her feet from the floor and hurried through the kitchen to Grandma's room. Grandpa was nowhere to be seen, but his old hat hung from a corner of the mirror. Did Patricia have him, too?

She crawled across the bed to the little table on Grandma's side. The drawer revealed medication, tissues, a pair of reading glasses, but no book. Below, in the cabinet section, she found several books. She was about to ask which one when she found the one Grandma meant. She was sure of it.

The book was old, older than the ones in her library. Older than Grandma, older than the house, older even, she would guess, that the woods themselves. The cover appeared to be made of tanned hide of some sort, but it was cracked and weathered. The pages within seemed thicker than paper, more sturdy. She had no doubt it was the book Grandma meant.

A crash and a scream came from the living room, followed by eerie silence. Hadley crept across the bedroom to the doorway.

"Grandma?" Her voice came out as a whisper, the squeak of a tiny mouse in a cage. "Grandma?"

There was no answer.

Her breath came in hitches as she slowly crossed the kitchen. Every step, she looked into corners and peered beneath the table to make sure nothing and no one hid beneath it. As she passed the cutting board, she pulled the biggest knife from the block. The pantry door stood ajar, and she took a good look inside, but there was nothing. Only preserves, boxes of crackers, and a few boxes of mac and cheese. The veil around Grandma's library was down, the spell broken. The books lay scattered across the floor, pages torn out and spines broken.

As she came to the doorway on the other side of the kitchen, her heart pounded. A single frightened tear rolled down her cheek, but she didn't care about it. She put the hand with the knife on the door, gulped air, and pushed.

"Grandma?"

The room was just as it had been, without any obvious source of the crash. But Grandma was gone. She couldn't be, but she was.

"Grandma!"

More running footsteps overhead, followed by giggling.

"You don't have to be lonely," said Patricia's voice. "Come play with me. I'm coming to play with you."

The footsteps ran toward the stairs, growing louder with each step until it sounded like whatever walked on those feet was gigantic. Hadley turned and ran out of the house onto the porch and slammed the door behind her, then she ran toward the tree line. It didn't matter that she didn't know where she was going or even what was out there. What mattered was getting away from the house, away from Patricia, and finding someplace she could hide until she could figure out what to do.

The veil around the house was gone, lifted like the one in front of Grandma's library, and Hadley found herself running through the woods, dodging trees, and ducking under branches, jumping roots and tripping over little hills. She ran until her lungs burned and her legs ached, then she stumbled to her knees, dropped the book and the kitchen knife, and sobbed.

CHAPTER TEN

Hadley sat in on the dirty forest floor until her body hitched from trying to cry with no more tears to shed. The twins were gone, and so was Grandma. Grandpa too, though she never saw what happened to him. For all she knew, Patricia had him.

Patricia pretended to be her friend then broke into Grandma's house.

No, that was wrong. She didn't break in. Hadley invited her.

But what about the boys? They walked right across the yard and into the woods, something that they would never do. But she saw them, clear as daylight, as they disappeared beyond the veil. And Grandma... One moment she was there, the next there was a scream and she was gone. Where could Patricia have taken her so quickly? It didn't make sense. Then again, nothing did. Not the house, the veil, not even why Mom would drop them off in such a place.

It didn't even make sense why she would run off into the woods. Grandma said the woods were dangerous, that the house was the only safe place. But the house didn't seem very safe anymore, and she didn't know her way around the woods at all. There was no "safe" place for her. The only thing she knew to do was try to go back to the house and find Grandma's phone to call Mom. Mom would know what to do. She had to.

Hadley pushed herself off the ground and picked up the book and the knife from where they lay. The book might not be much help, but it was Grandma's, and somehow holding it made her feel just the tiniest bit better. The knife wasn't particularly useful to her either, as she didn't know how to use it, but it was better than nothing. The best thing she could do was to take it in steps.

Step one, get back to the house.

Step two, find the phone and call Mom.

She looked around in the darkness to see if there was anything she recognized, any indication of even from which direction she came. But there was nothing. To her, the trees all looked alike, and without street signs, her navigation skills were nonexistent. But she couldn't have run more than a few yards. The easiest thing to do would be to walk for a few minutes in one direction, and if that one wasn't right, walk back and try another. It seemed simple enough. All she had to do was mark her current location with something so she would know when she got back. But what? She had a book and a knife, and Grandma told her that the trees wouldn't appreciate being carved upon. There was also no way she was going to leave Grandma's book. Instead, she searched the forest floor until she found a large fallen branch. The trees couldn't possibly mind if she carved on something already fallen.

She made a mark with the knife, jammed the stick into the ground, then chose a direction and walked. Twenty steps, and there was nothing familiar. Only more trees, more darkness. She turned around and walked back until she found her stick as she'd left it, then walked the opposite direction. Twenty more steps. Ahead, a stick protruded from the ground, carved with her symbol. It couldn't be. She'd just came from it. She couldn't have walked in a circle.

She turned and ran back in the direction she came. Her stick was there, marked. But so was another. And another.

Giggles flitted through the stagnant air.

"It's not funny," she shouted. "What do you want?"

Come play, said the voice.

"I don't want to play! I want my brothers and my grandparents back!"

Come and get them, giggled the voice. *They're waiting.*

Hadley sat down again in a huff. Patricia was there, watching. It was all some sick game, and she didn't want to play. But she didn't really have a choice. If she wanted them back, she'd have to go and find them herself.

She was about to say as much when a small ball of light appeared in the forest.

Don't say anything. The voice was familiar, but she couldn't put a name to it. *I can guide you out. You have to trust me.*

It was nothing like the rest of the forest, dark and terrifying. The light was blue and cool, but the voice that came out of it was warm like a fuzzy blanket.

Please, said the voice. *Trust me.*

She nodded and stood, then slowly walked toward the bobbing orb of light.

Hurry, it said. *There's not much time.*

Hadley picked up the pace and followed. It darted through the trees, under logs and over roots, until she came to a place she recognized. The grey wall of mist that surrounded Grandma's house was back, thicker than before. The veil.

Hurry, said the voice. *We have to close it before she comes back.*

She ran through, ignoring the feeling of spiderwebs on her face that the veil left. The ball of light waited on the porch, where it shimmered and changed form.

"Grandpa!"

The old man looked sad and tired as he slumped to the floor of the porch.

"I'm sorry," he said. "I haven't had to do that for a long time."

"What happened to you? How'd you do that?"

"We need to get into the house," he said. "I'll tell you when we're safe. Then we need to find your grandmother and your brothers. But first things first."

He rose to his considerable height, faced the yard, and set himself into a strong stance.

"You are not welcome here," he bellowed. "I rescind the invitation! You were invited under false pretense, and this house affords you safe haven no longer! You can come no further than the edge of the veil!"

A cold wind blew from somewhere in the forest, and on it came a giggle.

You can't rescind an invitation you didn't give, said Patricia, though she was nowhere to be seen. *Silly old man. It's not your house. I can come and go as I please.*

"I was afraid of that," said Grandpa. "You're going to have to do it." He leveled his gaze at Hadley.

"Do what?"

"You have to rescind the invitation," he said. "Just do it like I did and it should be fine."

She stared at him for a moment. Two weeks ago, she might've thought he was crazy. But two weeks ago, magic wasn't real and neither were weird creatures that pretended to be nice little girls in the woods. In light of everything that had happened in the last hour, she was in no position to argue what was and wasn't real.

Hadley mimicked her grandfather's stance, looked to him one more time, then swallowed the lump in her chest.

"You're not my friend!" The wind picked up and howled in her face. "You don't get to come over anymore! I rescind my invitation! You're not my summer sister!"

The wind dropped so quickly, she almost fell from leaning into it, but the giggle that rode its back still echoed through the air.

"That's got her for now," said Grandpa. "We're safe. But we need to get inside. We gotta figure out how to save your brothers and Grandma."

"How'd you do that?"

Hadley sat at the kitchen table, a cup of cocoa in her hand and a blanket around her shoulders. Although the summer night was warm, she couldn't chase the chill out of her bones.

"Grandma was teaching you magic," he said. "I've got a little bit of my own, though not as much as I used to have when I was..."

His voice trailed off. Something in his expression nipped at her heart, such pain in his eyes that she couldn't imagine what would hurt so badly.

"When you were... what? What are you?"

"I'm your grandfather," he said. "Or I was. I think I still am. I hope I still am."

"Of course, you are," she said. "What else would you be? But what was that out there?"

"Patricia," he said. "She's been trying to get into this house for a long time. Ever since she stole your mother's little sister and tried to replace her."

"She's a changeling?"

"I believe so," said Grandpa.

"Everything Grandma said was true?"

"'Fraid so." He shrugged and sat down. "That's why she was teaching you magic. The world needs more people who know magic and can use it. But it's dangerous. That's why she teaches it way out here, away from everyone else, and has all them rules. But..."

"But I broke them," said Hadley, tears welling in her eyes and a lump in her throat. "And now they're gone, and it's my fault."

"They ain't gone," said Grandpa. "Not yet. You can still get them back. All of them."

"Me? How?"

"Grandma's been teaching you, hasn't she?"

"Yes." But she'd taught her how to conjure a match flame, or how to turn her eyes blue, or what plant could make a headache go away. She didn't teach her anything about fighting monsters. That lesson must've been meant for later.

"You got that book of Grandma's?"

The old book sat on the table, its cover worn and stained.

"It's got everything in it that you need. You just need some learnin' up."

"What about you? You know about all of this stuff. Why don't you help me?"

"I can't." He gave a sad smile. "I wish I could, but I can't."

For a moment she stared at him. He had the knowledge, but he wouldn't help?

"Is this why Mom won't talk to you anymore? Because you wouldn't help?"

His face dropped, and he stood to leave.

"Your mother is mad at me for something I did, not something I didn't do."

"And what was that?"

"I died."

He said it quietly, so much so that she wasn't sure she'd heard him correctly. But he didn't clarify, didn't even look at her. He'd said it, and he meant it.

"What're you talking about? You're standing right here."

In answer, Grandpa disappeared, popped out of existence like a soap bubble, then back again in the same place. Were it not for the situation, Hadley would probably have laughed.

"How long?"

"Almost two years now," he said. "Died in the winter. That's why I'm always gathering firewood. Your Grandma kept the place up. We were supposed to leave here, find some nice little cottage somewhere and forget this place. But we couldn't. Not with that thing still out there. It took our daughter, left your mom without a sister. She still blames herself. That's why she didn't teach you about magic. She's lost her confidence in it. She lost her spark."

"I'm sorry," said Hadley. "I didn't know."

"You weren't supposed to," said Grandpa. "You were supposed to learn the family ways and never come into contact with that thing. But now she's claimed your brothers, just like she took our Patricia."

"And you can't do anything about this?"

"You heard her," said Grandpa. "I don't even exist anymore. I'm just a shadow. I'm nothing to her."

"So it's on me."

He nodded.

"You can still help me," said Hadley. "You may be dead, but you can help me with your knowledge."

"Whatever I can do to help, I will."

The book was old, older even than the most worn of the journals in Grandma's library. And while the pages looked strange and thick, they fairly crackled with power. There was no name in the front of the book to reveal its author, but the pages were hand-written in faded ink. Many pages in, the hand switched to one younger or more firm.

"That book's been in your Grandma's family for a long time," said Grandpa. "It was old when it was passed to her. Every generation that's held it has added a section. Your

Grandma was transcribing it, trying to make sense out of some of the pages."

"How's this supposed to help me?" She flipped pages back and forth. "There's no index or anything."

"Call out what you want to know about," said Grandpa. "Nice and firm. Remember how Grandma told you about intention? Direct your intention to the book."

Hadley focused on the book, pictured her energy as a current of water from her core flowing through her hands and onto the pages.

"Changelings," she said.

For a moment, nothing happened. Then, the book was taken by an almost imperceptible tremor. The tremor became a shake, then the book opened where it sat and pages fanned past. When it came to a rest, it lay open on a page she'd have never found on her own. The entry "Changeling" was written in large script across the top of the page. Below was an illustration of human-shaped shadow without distinguishing characteristics.

"There's no picture," said Grandpa over her shoulder. "They can look like whatever they want, so there's no point."

"Makes sense," said Hadley. "But what do they really look like?"

"No one knows," said Grandpa.

"Changelings," read Hadley. "They hate iron and are only vulnerable in their true form."

"All woods creatures hate iron. They get their strength from the woods, y'see?" Grandpa sat in the chair across from her and fidgeted. "Take 'em out of the woods, they die off."

"Okay," said Hadley. "So, how do I get one in its true form?"

"Dunno," said Grandpa. "I suppose the big issue is to find it first."

"I don't think that'll be a problem," said Hadley. "It keeps calling to me to play with it."

"It does?" A look of concern crossed his face. "It bonded with you. That's bad. It's not going to stop until it gets what it wants, and that's you."

A stone settled in her stomach. What could it possibly want with her? Not even a week ago, she didn't even know things like changelings existed. For one to be so determined to get her seemed impossible.

"So, what do I do?"

Her grandfather's face wavered a bit, the first time she'd seen him for the ghost he was.

"The way I see it," he said. "You got two choices. You could run, and ain't nobody would blame you if you did.

Or you can fight and maybe lose all your future days to that thing."

"What would you do?"

Grandpa's face sank.

"I done it," he said. "I tried to fight, but it was too late. It cost me my youngest child, and it cost your mother her sister. Patty was dead and weren't nothing I could do to fix it."

"Patty? You mean *Patricia?*"

Grandpa nodded. "It looks just like she did the day we buried her."

A tiny coal of anger flickered to life in her chest. That *thing* was running around the forest wearing a stolen face, one that was designed to hurt her grandparents. Designed to taunt her mother. She wasn't going to let the same thing happen to her brothers or her grandmother.

"Okay," she said. "Tell me everything you know."

PART TWO

BEYOND THE VEIL

The woods are lovely dark and deep.
But I have promises to keep,
And miles to go before I sleep,
And miles to go before I sleep.
From *Stopping by Woods on a Snowy Evening,* by Robert
Frost

CHAPTER ELEVEN

Hadley felt more like a soldier than a kid as she stepped off the porch. Although she wore pink sneakers instead of combat boots, and denim overall-shorts were her only body armor, it would have to do. Grandma's magic lessons left her feeling unprepared, and she had only a few meager items in her backpack, but as she stared at the veil, she clung to what few weapons she had as if they could really protect her.

Grandpa had helped her prepare. He couldn't go with her, he'd said, and couldn't really do anything if he could. He wasn't strong enough to affect the physical world outside the veil. It was only inside the wall her Grandma had built that the illusion of life was still convincing. Outside, Hadley would be able to see him, but it would be as if he were a puff of Grandpa-shaped smoke. She wouldn't even be able to hear his voice. Still, in the house, he helped her load a backpack with things he was sure she'd need, all the while telling her important details about what she was sure to encounter in the woods.

She tried to listen, tried to remember every word. But after a while, it all ran together in frantic gibberish. She didn't know the difference between a hobgoblin and a brownie, didn't know what to do if a Puckwudgie crossed her path, or even what she would do against the changeling if she found it. Grandma hadn't gotten to that part of the lessons yet. Still, she couldn't just sit around doing nothing. Her brothers were her responsibility, and it was her fault Patricia had come into the house in the first place. If she'd have just followed the rules, none of this would've happened.

"Above everything else," said Grandpa. "Remember these four things. You've got Grandma's book of lore. That's got all kinds of stuff about woods-folk in it. You've got a big bag of salt, and that'll ward off most anything. You've got magic that Grandma taught you, and it may not seem like much, but it can come in handy. And finally..." He raised a silver whistle to her eye level. "You feel like you can't go on anymore, you blow this. I'll hear it, and I'll guide you home. Do you have your key?"

Hadley raised it around her neck.

"That'll get you back in past the veil around the yard. Never had to lock it before because we didn't think we needed it."

She flinched.

"But now that we do," he continued as if he didn't notice. "It works just like the one around the library. You can get through. Whoever you're holding onto can get through. But anything else that holds magic can't get through. Period."

"So the changeling won't be able to follow?"

"No," said Grandpa. "At least, I hope not. But then, we thought that before, didn't we?"

"I don't know if I can do this," she said.

"You have to," said Grandpa. "It's you or nobody. Without you, they're lost for good."

"Aren't you supposed to be trying to talk me out of this? Like it's too dangerous or something?"

Grandpa paused, as if he'd not considered it before.

"Why? Do you think I could?"

Hadley thought for a moment, then let out a heavy sigh.

"No," she said. "I want my brothers back. I want Grandma back. And it's my fault they're gone."

"Now, honey..."

"No," she said again. "Even if I wanted to go to the police or someone, no one would believe me. It has to be me. Like you said, it's me or nobody."

"Well, then," said Grandpa. He bent down and kissed her on the forehead and then traced a star where the kiss was. "You be careful. I don't want to lose you, too."

"You won't," she said, though she wished she was as confident as she sounded.

Hadley turned back toward the house for a moment. Grandpa stood in the window, a sad smile on his face as he waved. She nodded, waved back, then turned and walked toward the veil in a straight line, eyes fixed on a tree. If she let herself look around, she might lose her resolve, might realize just how scared she was, then she'd run back into the house and never come out again. But she couldn't. Her brothers, Grandma, needed her. And she wasn't just some twelve-year-old girl in pink sneakers with a backpack on her back. She was a witch from a long line of witches. She had magic at her command. Grandpa had helped her fill her backpack with things she could use to fight, including the big bag of salt. She also had Grandma's book, a tin full of iron nails, a roll of kite string, a paper bag full of red brick dust, and a velvet sack full of cut glass and plastic gems. Around her waist was a leather belt from which dangled Grandpa's old hunting knife.

Grandma had power enough to create the veil and to call fire whenever she wanted, and who knew what else? And what was she really but just a girl. But then, she thought of her brothers, holding hands and frightened somewhere in the dark with Patricia looming over them, and anger overtook her fear. She hurried to the edge of the veil then stopped. Before she knew what it was, she looked right past it without a second thought. The workings Grandmother had woven into it were simple but elegant. It was made so that, unless one knew she was looking at it, she wouldn't see it. But now that she knew what it was, she couldn't help but see the rippling distortion in space, the wall that stood between the woods and Grandmother's house. She looked upward and realized that it went higher than she could easily see.

She turned back for a moment, doubt wrapping around her innards like a snake. Grandpa still watched from the window, his face a mask of worry. But he smiled and waved, raised a single thumb in the air. Hadley nodded and stepped through the veil.

The air on the other side of the veil was still, as hot and wet as a swamp. As soon as the wall closed behind her, she began to sweat. The trail she and Patricia had taken was gone, as if it had never been there at all. But Hadley recognized a fallen log, a few rocks, and set off on her way, careful to be quiet as she walked. Grandpa told her that the wood-folk were solitary creatures, but that they were drawn to noise, and it was in her best interest to keep as quiet as possible. Although she tried, every step she took seemed to echo with the crunch of dead leaves and the crack of fallen twigs and sticks. Grandma's yard was covered in lush green grass that was soft under bare feet. But the ground here was dirt and debris, pebbles and bark. The woods held its breath, like it knew a fight was coming.

The problem was, she wasn't sure where to go. The old shack with Patricia's things in them, what Grandpa called her "horde," seemed like a good place to start. But the farther she walked, the less familiar the woods looked, and it wasn't long before she had to admit she was lost.

A downed tree made a good place to rest for a bit while she tried to figure out where she was and how to get where she needed to go.

She opened her backpack and looked inside. Of all the things she brought, Grandpa didn't think to include water or food. Maybe he'd been a ghost for too long and didn't remember what it was like to be hungry or thirsty.

Grandma's book was by far the heaviest thing in the pack, but she didn't dare leave it. Grandpa said it had all of her knowledge about the woods and what was in them. He called it a "grimoire," but it didn't look very grim to her. Old, maybe, but not grim.

Hadley placed the book on the log in front of her and then closed her eyes and held her hand over it. Then, she pictured her own power flowing out of her hands like water onto the book.

"I'm lost," she said.

The pages flipped open as if directed by wind. When they came to a rest, the words on the page were in a faded script she could barely make out.

This is my journey. And every journey begins with but a single step.

On the opposite page in darker ink were the words "Finding Your Way." She spread the book open across her lap and read. It seemed like a spell, but in plain language that was easy to understand. No rhymes or fancy words. In fact, it was written just the way Grandma talked.

"Take an iron nail," it said. In her mind, Grandma's voice spoke. "And wrap it twelve times with a piece of string, then tie it off. Once it's good and tight, hang it down from a piece of string as long as your arm and think real hard about where you want to go."

Seemed simple enough. She dug through her backpack and pulled out the little tin. Inside there were more than a dozen rusty nails. She picked a big heavy red one, then she pulled out the kite string. As she followed the directions carefully, she whispered.

"I need to find the shack. I need to find the shack. I need to find the shack."

When she was done, Hadley used the knife from her belt to cut the string and held it out in front of her, eyes closed as she concentrated on the place she needed to go. The shack. The dirt floor covered with a dirty blanket. The toys. The lost items. All of it. She needed to find it, needed the magic to guide her.

When she opened her eyes, the nail was spinning like mad at the end of the string. She scarcely breathed as it slowed, changed direction, then changed again. After a moment, the pointed end froze, the direction marked and clear.

"Thanks, Grandma," she said as she set off through the trees.

Branches overhead blocked out most of the sunlight. Enough came through to light her way, but the woods were dark. It gave a strange sense of artificial twilight, to walk among the shadowy trees and underbrush. Strange that it never seemed so dark when she and Patricia were playing. But maybe that had more to do with the changeling than anything else.

The nail stayed pointed toward what she hoped was her destination, but it pointed only in a straight line. More than once, it led her straight into a tree or through a rock. She had to back up and go around, every step carefully chosen so as not to trip in the dimness. But the nail continued to point. When she turned, it adjusted. When she stopped, it tugged at the string. How it knew where she was going, she could only guess was part of the magic Grandma taught. But if what Grandma said was true, and all magic had a cost, she wondered what the cost of this spell would be. However, it was in Grandma's book, and she trusted Grandma, so she put her trust in the nail at the end of the string.

After a while, the darkness grew thicker as the sun began its descent. Strange that it didn't take her nearly so long to get to the little shack with Patricia in the lead. But the nail kept pointing the same direction. It was as if the woods grew and shifted in a game of hide-and-seek to keep her from reaching her goal. She stopped and sat, tired and frustrated.

She'd find them. She had to. She couldn't just let Patricia keep them.

Behind her, past a cluster of bushes, came a rustling sound accompanied by a voice. As quietly as she could, she crept from her seat and peered through the bushes.

A few yards away, a hollow log sat jammed into the ground, one end pointed to the sky. Out of the skyward end, a pair of legs, filthy and hairy, kicked dirty feet. With every kick, the man's volume increased, as did his anger, but she couldn't understand a word he said.

"Hello?"

The kicking stopped.

"Who's out there?" It was more a demand than a question.

"Are you okay?"

"Do I *look* okay?" The legs flailed harder. "I'm stuck's what I am."

"Can I help?"

"I don't know," came the angry voice from inside the log. "Can you?"

Since she had no reply, Hadley stepped up to the tree. The man's legs were smaller than she thought, though his feet were enormous.

"How'd you get stuck in there?"

"Chasing a rabbit," he said. "Was going to have it for dinner."

She took hold of his muddy ankles and pulled.

"GAH! Not like that! What're you trying to do, pull my legs off?"

"I'm sorry! I'm trying!"

"Try different!"

Hadley set her shoulders, put one foot on the lip of the log, and pulled again. The little man shouted in pain, but after a moment, he popped free, and he and Hadley rolled to the forest floor. When he stood, she couldn't believe her eyes.

The creature was no more a man than she was. In fact, despite the size of its legs, it came up only to just above her chest. From the back, it resembled a hedgehog, but when it turned around, it was very different. Its wiry muscled arms and legs seemed to jut directly from its oversized head with a pair of kite-shaped ears for good measure. The whole of it was obscured in long hair and reeds, except for its banana-shaped nose and the twinkling silver eyes that peered from beneath bushy brows.

It scrambled to its feet, brushed off its front, then turned and looked at her.

"Oh," he said, distaste evident. "You're one of *them*."

"What's that supposed to mean? 'Them' who?"

"People," he said.

"Aren't you a person?"

"Certainly not!" he roared. If he had a chest, he'd have puffed it out, but his glittering eyes bored into her. "We, and all the others like me, are *folk*. That's all. Your *people* are the ones who gave us your own stupid names. Take me. *People* can't wrap their mouths around what my folk are called, so they gave us their own name. Puckwudgie. Now I ask you, does that sound respectful?"

The way he said the word "people" offended and fascinated her. It was as if the word had taste, and it was a bad one. Every time he said it, it seemed like spoiled milk and orange juice across his tongue. She shook her head.

"*People* called us that so much that it stuck, and now no one can remember what we're really called, so now we're puckwudgies. *People* done come to our woods, took our homes, and for what? Those big ugly caves they live in? Feh!"

"I'm sorry," she said. "I've never met any folk before. I didn't know."

"Meh," he said. "You ain't a very big people. And you helped me out. Name's Gristle."

He stuck a mud- and moss-covered hand out. She took it without a second thought.

"Hadley," she said.

"Funny sort of name," said Gristle. "What sorta thing is a Hadley? An' what're you doing out here?"

"A changeling took my family."

She sat down on the hollow log as she told him the story. When she was done, he stared at her for a moment.

"Woods ain't safe for a people," he said. "Especially one so small as you."

"I can't go back without them," she said. "I want my family back."

He seemed to consider, then climbed up on the hollow log and reached inside. From out of it he pulled a bow and small quiver of arrows.

"You helped me," said Gristle. "That means I got a debt needs repaying. I'm gonna help you."

"I'd like that," she said. "Right now, I'm lost."

"Harumph," said Gristle. "Lost ain't nothing. Lost becomes found pretty quick. Where's this Patricia at?"

"I don't know," said Hadley. "But I'm trying to find her shack where she keeps stuff she finds. I'm using this nail—"

Gristle stepped back at the sight of it.

"That thing's iron," he whispered. "Can't none of us folk be touched by iron. Put it away. Put it away!"

She tucked it into her pocket.

"Besides," he said as he regained his composure. "Don't need no spell no more. You got me."

She didn't really know him, had no reason to trust him, but a guide would be better than a magic nail on a string. Besides, his proclamation that he'd help made her feel better, less alone.

"I don't even know you," she said.

"You can trust me."

She considered for a moment.

"Swear it," she said. "Promise me you'll help me find my family."

"I swear it," said Gristle, his hand raised. "By the root and soil."

"I don't know what that means," said Hadley.

Gristle lowered his hand and looked at her as if he'd never heard such a thing, then he lowered his eyes.

"On the lives of my wife and young'uns, I'll help you find your family."

There was such emotion in his voice that she couldn't help but believe him. If the strange creature was determined to be an ally, she'd welcome him. After all, magic or no, she was only a child, and she could use all the help she could get. She smiled and got to her feet.

"Lead the way," she said.

CHAPTER TWELVE

Gristle moved over the rocks faster than she thought possible for his odd body. No matter the terrain, he made climbing over or around look easy. At times, Hadley struggled to keep up. Every time she lost sight of him for a few moments, terror struck her spine. What if he just left her out in the woods, so far away from Grandma's house, all alone? But every time, she found him waiting for her at the next ridge.

"Hurry up!" he growled. "Stupid *people* legs. Stupid *people* feet. No good for climbing or running, you ask me."

Even though she moved as fast as she could, and she had longer legs than the puckwudgie, she couldn't keep up. His toes found every gripping place while her sneakers slipped and slid. More than once she fell but scrambled to her feet to try to keep up with Gristle.

"Enough!" she said at last. "I have to sit and rest for a minute! You're too fast, and I can't keep up."

She dropped to the forest floor and shrugged off her backpack. Gristle reappeared in front of her and hurried to her side.

"What're you doing?"

"Resting," she said. "Or don't folk rest?"

"We do when it's time for resting," he said. "And this ain't no time for that. Bits and bobs, girl, don't you know where you is?"

"I'm in the woods," she said. "Chasing a puckwudgie to find my Grandma and my brothers, who were kidnapped by a changeling. Of course, I know where I am."

"No," said Gristle. "I mean *right now*. Don't you know nothing?"

"Where am I, then?"

"You's in the woods," he said. "That's true. But you's in a whole n'other kingdom now. It's a kingdom of folk, and they doesn't like people. Not one bit."

"Are there any around?"

"Well... No," he said.

"Then I'm resting," she replied. "I can't keep going so fast. You'll lose me."

He stared at her for a moment then threw his hands up.

"Fine," he said. "You rest. I'll go look up ahead, see what's what up there. Just don't take too long."

Hadley was about to reply, but he sprinted off through the underbrush, and she was alone.

Without Gristle to keep her attention, she took a good look around. Every tree, to her, looked the same. The ground on which she walked could've been the same space just outside the veil at Grandma's house. To her, a rock was a rock and a tree was a tree. If she lost Gristle, she'd have no way of knowing where she was. She'd either have to rely on the iron nail or blow the whistle and wait for Grandpa to get her, then she'd have to start over.

She opened her backpack and took out Grandma's book and thumbed through. Without the spell, it was like a cookbook, with recipes, pictures, and stories, but it had no discernable order. The spell was the easiest way to find information in the book. It would be better, she reckoned, to read the thing in its entirety, cover to cover, so she didn't miss anything. But that could wait until later.

Hadley flipped through the pages until she found a sketch that looked very much like her companion next to an entry labeled "Puckwudgies." According to the book, they were once friendly to humans, until the humans did something unforgivable. It didn't say what, but it was apparent that whatever it was created a massive rift between the two species, one that couldn't be bridged. She read further until a single line stopped her.

Puckwudgies are not to be trusted. Beside it, in Grandma's unmistakable hand, was the word "Gristle."

Grandma knew him. She closed the book and put it back in her pack, then she stood and dusted herself off. Whether Grandma trusted him or not, he was still her best hope of finding them. Sure, the nail could guide her, but he could do it faster. Hadley had to trust him. She didn't have much of a choice. But she needed to keep a close eye on him. If the book, and maybe Grandma, said he wasn't to be trusted, then he wasn't to be trusted.

She moved in the direction she'd last seen Gristle but didn't see him up ahead.

"Gristle!" She quickened her pace. "Gristle! Where are you?"

Not even the wind replied. The branches overhead were silent, and not a single creature moved in the underbrush. Hadley turned in a circle, but there were no distinguishing landmarks, no hints as to where she was. After a moment, she'd forgotten which direction she was headed and was, again, lost.

She reached into her pocket and pulled out the nail on the string. So what if he'd just left her alone? She didn't need him to guide her. In fact, she was doing just fine before Gristle showed up stuck in the log. She helped him because it was the right thing to do, not so he would be in debt to her. Besides, what had he really done for her besides walk her around in circles for hours?

She held the nail in her hand and closed her eyes.

But what if he was hurt? What if something else happened to him? He was folk, and folk knew the woods. Maybe she didn't need him, but maybe she did.

She let the nail drop to the end of the string and then pictured liquid energy flowing down her arm toward the nail.

"Find Gristle," she said. "Find Gristle the puckwudgie."

When she opened her eyes, the nail spun, then slowed, then stopped and pointed.

The problem with walking through the woods was that Hadley had no sense of time. At twelve years old, the concept of "time" was more a product of whether or not she was enjoying the activity at hand. School was a torturous eight-hour day that seemed endless, while books she could devour and swear only a few moments had passed, though her mother told her that hours had gone by.

However long the time was, Hadley wasn't having fun.

The nail pointed, turned, then pointed again. She followed its directions until she came to a clearing in the woods. It appeared to be circular, with a ring of mushrooms growing through the center. She'd seen them in Austin often and never given such a thing a second thought, but Grandma told her what it was, a faery ring, and that she should be wary of it. But she didn't know why.

The nail pointed upward. She wound it in the string and pocketed it before she looked up.

Above the faery ring hung a bag that looked like it was woven out of long reeds. The way it bulged and pitched, it was easy to guess what, or rather who, was inside.

"Gristle!"

She ran into the clearing before she could think.

Screams came from all sides, followed by howls and whistles. Something pricked her leg. She drew back in surprise, only to find a tiny quill sticking out of her sock. The bare parts of her legs, however, held several of the slivers.

"Run, child!" screamed the bag. "Don't let 'em catch you!"

She turned and darted back toward the tree line. Even though there were a dozen new prickles on her legs, she couldn't see their source. The tiny whooping voices gave her the idea that, although she couldn't see them, there were dozens of assailants.

As she reached the edge of the clearing, something snagged her ankles and wrapped her feet up tight. She toppled and fell flat on her face onto the leafy forest floor. When she looked up, she realized why she couldn't see her assailants.

They were tiny.

Dozens of tiny folk, each dressed in leaves and what appeared to be the skins of mice, ran along the branches of the trees above. None of them were any taller than a few inches, and all of them carried weapons.

She looked down at her feet. Around her ankles were ropes made from long grass and reeds with nuts on the ends to give them weight. As she reached for them, the folk in the trees shrieked a war cry and leaped down at her.

"Don't move!" shouted the one who landed on her chest. He wore the skull of a mouse as a helmet and brandished a spear not much bigger than a toothpick, while the four that stood on either side of him held bows with arrows nocked.

"Brownie scum!" shouted the bag. "Leave'er alone! She ain't done nothing to you!"

Brownies. For a moment, she forgot that she was tied up and marveled that the tiny creatures were real. Grandma had talked about them, of course, but she always assumed they were just more of Grandma's fantastical world of the woods, yarns that she spun to keep her and her brothers entertained.

But they were real enough and armed to their tiny teeth.

"Please!" said Hadley. "I didn't mean to do anything wrong!"

The brownies in the trees twittered in another language all their own that she had neither the education nor the faculties to understand. Some of the words sounded like the chirp of cicadas at night, others like bullfrogs in the darkness. How many times, she wondered, had they been all around, but she'd never known? The one with the mouse helmet made a sound like a blue jay, and the others went silent.

"You *people* never mean to do wrong," he said as he jabbed at her nose with his spear. "But you do wrong all the time. You stepped into a holy place without an offering, and you expect us to let you go?"

"I'm sorry," she said. "I didn't know. What sort of offering?"

"One that shows your good intent," said the brownie. "That shows your reverence for folk."

"Like what?"

"Riches!" shouted the brownie, much to the delight of those that still sat in trees. "Honey! Tea! What you *people* call, uh, chocolate!"

"I don't have any of those things," she said. "I didn't know I'd need them."

From above, brownies chirped like birds in laughter.

"What would it take to let us both go?" The brownies went quiet again.

"You?" said the leader. "You don't know better than to stomp all over the ground. Restitution must be paid, then you turn around and go back where you came from. But him?" He jerked a thumb to the wriggling sack above the faery ring. "He knows better. He broke the covenant. We won't let him go."

"But I need him," she said.

"Don't matter. He broke the covenant."

"Stupid covenant!" The bag wriggled harder. "Folk go where they please!"

"What do you mean, restitution? I don't have anything."

"Everybody's got something," said the leader. "You may not think of it as valuable, but everything's valuable to someone."

He nodded, and a dozen brownies pulled her backpack off her shoulders and dumped it on the ground. Then, they picked through the meager contents with their spears.

When one came to the zipper bag, it was a strain for his tiny body to pull the zipper open. Once so, he stood back and gasped. The others rushed over and made sounds like crickets. The leader joined them, looked inside, then climbed back onto Hadley' chest.

"We didn't know you were so wealthy," he said. "Untie her!"

The brownies did as their leader asked and then backed slowly away as she got to her feet.

"Surely, a queen such as yourself means no harm to the brownie folk," said the leader as he removed his helmet. "The accords are between our people and other folk. One who carries iron and salt, who has a purse full of jewels, has no need to hurt the brownies."

Slowly, their meaning dawned on her. The iron nails, the bag of salt, all of them could harm the brownies. From their point of view, she must look like a traveling marauder. The zipper bag full of cut glass and plastic they must've taken for jewels.

"I don't want to hurt anyone," said Hadley. "And I didn't mean to trespass. If you want the jewels, take them. I just want my friend down from that bag."

The leader's eyes grew wide. He made a few bird-like sounds, and half-dozen brownies picked up the zipper bag and hurried away with it. Another half dozen climbed the tree and cut the rope that held the bag suspended. It hit the ground with a thump.

"Why does he matter to you?" The leader put his helmet back on. "Puckwudgie are nothing but trouble. They don't trust your kind, and your kind can't trust them."

"He's helping me," she said. "I need him to help me find my family. I don't expect you to understand."

"What happened to them?"

"They were taken," she said. "By a changeling."

At the utterance of the word, the woods went silent.

"We know it," said the leader. "And it knows us. If it took your family, leave them. It won't give them back."

A lump built in the pit of her stomach as she fought the tears that threatened to spill from her eyes.

"I can't," she said. "It has my brothers and my grandma. I can't just leave them. I have to try."

"Then please," said the leader. "Be careful. We brownies have to clean up what she leaves of her prey. I beg the gods that we don't have to clean you up as well."

The brownies took several steps backward and then turned and disappeared into the trees. For a moment, Hadley tried to track them, but she gave up when she realized it would be like tracking a mouse through a thicket.

"Nasty things, brownies." Gristle wriggled his way out of the bag then kicked it away. "Horrible, every last one of them."

"They let you go," said Hadley.

"Kept your bag of jewels," said Gristle. "Probably gave them more than they'd have asked for."

"They were worthless," she said. "Plastic and glass."

"Brownies don't care for money," he snapped. "They care how it sparkles. The more it shines like stars, the more they wants it. We needs to get going. Lots worse than brownies in the woods, and ain't all of it friendly to folk nor people."

CHAPTER THIRTEEN

Before, when Patricia took her to her little shed in the woods to see her treasures, it took only a few minutes to get there. But with every new step, the sunlight through the branches grew weaker, and it became clear that there was still a long walk ahead.

"I need to stop," she said. "And you need to slow down. It's getting too dark for me to see you."

"Forgot about that," said Gristle. "You *people* can't see none too good in the dark. Don't you have one of them things what shoots light?"

She hadn't thought to bring a flashlight. She'd assumed the journey would take only minutes, not hours. Certainly not past nightfall.

"No," she said.

"Best stop then," said Gristle. "For the best, I suppose. All manner of creature what don't like people nor folk in the woods at night."

As they weren't following a marked path, Gristle stopped and declared the place where they stood to be their camp until daylight, then he scampered into the underbrush. He returned moments later, his arms were loaded with dry twigs, which he piled together. From somewhere beneath his copious beard, he pulled stone and steel and went to work trying to set the tiny pile alight. With each failed attempt, his frustration became more evident.

"Root take it all," he shouted as he threw the flint to the ground. "Can't get none of this to light!"

"Let me," said Hadley.

"You?" Gristle scoffed. "What can a *people* like you do?"

For the first time in what seemed like days, Hadley felt that maybe she *could* be useful. She focused her will like Grandma taught her, then poured it out into the dry branch pile at her feet. For a moment, nothing happened. Then, a thin column of smoke rose from the twigs. Gristle stared wide-eyed as the kindling burst into flames.

"You didn't say nothing about knowing magic," he said. "You can do that, but you can't make light?"

"I only know a little," she said. "Grandma was teaching me."

"They's the same thing," said Gristle. "Just different."

"I don't understand."

"If you can do that, you can do lots more too. You may not know how, but you can do it. Now, help me feed this. Got to keep it burning. Keep the nasties away at night. Most of 'em, anyways."

Hadley didn't like the way he said *most of 'em*, but she didn't ask what he meant. Whatever the answer, she was certain she wouldn't like it. The two of them piled larger sticks on the fire until it was strong enough, then they sat and enjoyed the warmth and light. Hadley should've been exhausted, but the thought of sleeping in the woods, now that she knew that creatures like puckwudgies and brownies were real, seemed impossible. Instead, she put her back to the fire and took out her grandma's book.

"What's that you got there?"

"It's Grandma's," said Hadley. "It's got spells and things about all the folk as well."

"Oh?" he scoffed. "Lessee what it says about me."

Hadley flipped pages until she found the drawing that looked strikingly similar to the little creature in front of her. Then, before he saw it, she covered his name with her hand and read the entry.

"According to this, your kind can appear and disappear at will, often lure people to their deaths, and can use magic. It also says that your arrows are poisonous and that you can create fire."

"Hogwash," said Gristle. "Can't use magic, though we wishes we could. And ain't no poison on my arrows. And it looks like you make fire better'n me."

"It also says that you were once allies to people, but not anymore."

"Got that right," said Gristle. "People ain't no good for my kind. People ain't trustworthy, so we don't trust 'em."

"In that case," said Hadley. "Thank you for helping me. I really do appreciate it."

"Repaying a debt is all," said Gristle, then he turned and wandered back into the woods.

Hadley turned back toward the book. There was no index, no table of contents. Every page was a random smattering of information, each of the authors' minds laid out as they came to each thought. Grandpa said Grandma was trying to transcribe it. It was easy to see why.

She could use the indexing spell if she needed something specific, but just flipping through seemed like an endless barrage of information. There was nothing to do but start at the beginning and hope that whatever she read was useful, or skim until she found some relevant information. Every so often, the pages were dotted with pencil-sketched illustrations. Some were flowers with the usable parts labeled. Others, like that of the puckwudgie, were rough but accurate sketches of creatures. At least a few she found were diagrams of how to build some sort of apparatus, the purpose of which she didn't understand.

Hadley flipped through pages until she found a sketch that made her stop. In it, a girl with a book sat with her back to a large fire in the woods. On the other side of the fire, a tiny man stood. Beneath the sketch, Grandma had written "beware the shadows."

Each of the figures in the sketch had more than one shadow, several of which appeared to be looming over them. Several of them wore gleeful evil faces.

Hadley' heart raced. She wanted to look, to see how many shadows she had. But fear kept her eyes glued to the page. If there were more than one shadow, what was she to do? And besides, how dangerous could a shadow be?

There was nothing else on the page about them, apart from the cryptic warning. She closed the book and set it in her lap, then she took a deep breath and looked.

She had three shadows.

"Gristle!"

The puckwudgie appeared from out of the underbrush, his face stern for a moment. But when she pointed to the shadows on the ground, his eyes widened, and he looked quickly to the ground around him.

"I've got 'em too," he said. "Blast! Don't listen to anything they say!"

Sleep...

The voice followed a gentle breeze and cradled her mind in velvet.

You're so tired, it said. And the more she listened, the more she wanted to agree with it.

"Wretched darklings!" he shouted. "She ain't done nothing to you! Leave her alone!"

Shhhhhhhh...

Gristle's eyes went glassy, and he wavered then dropped to the ground.

"No!" The darklings attached to him moved from the dirt to his leathery feet, then slowly up his legs. "Leave him alone!"

From out of the trees came a pair of shrill cries. In the darkness, she couldn't see what made them, but they sounded the same as the war yelps of the brownies. Against the firelight, two brownies became clear, spears raised as they leaped from the boughs above. They stabbed at one of the darklings, and the air was filled with the sound of breaking glass and ice as the shadowy creature screamed.

"Iron!" screamed one of the brownies. "You have to pin them to the ground with iron! Then we can pull you free!"

Her heart raced as she grabbed her backpack and dumped it on the ground. The darklings attached to her climbed her legs. Wherever they touched, the skin burned cold, and the longer they held on, the more she felt lost, alone. All she wanted was sleep. She didn't care about her brothers or even Grandma anymore. None of it mattered. All she wanted was sleep.

"Don't give in!" A brownie climbed her sleeve and screamed in her ear, breaking the spell for a moment. She snatched up the little tin box and took out a nail, then she jammed it through one of the shadows attached to her foot. It immediately let go and shrieked.

"Hurry! Hurry!" The other brownie stabbed at the other shadows, who cried out but didn't let go. "Before it's too late!"

Hadley stabbed the other two shadows attached to her foot. Both of them cried out and writhed, but the nails kept them pinned to the ground. Both the brownies took hold of her shirt sleeves and strained, but she couldn't even feel them. If she was to get free, she'd have to do it herself. She reached behind and dug her fingers into the dirt, then pulled as hard as she could. Wherever the darkling touched, it stuck like hot tar. The harder she pulled, the more she couldn't be certain it wasn't taking pieces of her flesh off her legs with it. She screamed in agony as the last of the blackness snapped off her leg and left her in a crying heap on the leaf-strewn ground, then she struggled up to sitting and looked around.

"Gristle!"

The puckwudgie lay on the ground, his body covered in black sludge. The only thing that was not yet covered was his bulbous nose.

"We have to help him!"

"Too late for him," said one of the brownies. "At least we saved you, eh?"

"I'm not leaving him!"

Hadley ran to her fallen friend with the brownies close behind. As she pulled more nails from out of the tin, the tar around Gristle seemed to tighten.

"Careful!" said the brownie. "Don't get too close or it'll catch you again!"

She didn't care if it did. Gristle may have disliked people, but he was the first folk she'd met, and despite his gruff demeanor, she considered him a friend.

The creature shrieked as she drove a nail through it into the ground, but it didn't let go.

"We have to get it off of him!"

"We can't help him now," said one of the brownies. "The darklings have taken him."

But Hadley would not give up. She drove a second nail into the creature. It spasmed and retreated a little, uncovering Gristle's nostrils.

"It's no good," said the brownie. "It ain't letting go! The only other thing what can hurt a darkling is light!"

Gristle's words came back to her. *If you can do that, you can do lots more too. You may not know how, but you can do it.*

Hadley closed her eyes and pictured the power inside of her swirling like a whirlpool and then flowing out like Grandma showed her with fire. But instead of picturing flames, she pictured light, pictured everything around her lit up bright as day.

Pure white light erupted from her palms and bathed the darkling. Its oily surface smoked and sizzled as it shrieked and writhed. The brownies each pulled at Gristle's nose, but it did no good. Hadley drew her arm back as she prepared to hurl more light at the creature.

"I hope this doesn't hurt him," she said and then flung her arm forward.

Wherever light touched, it blistered and boiled. The darkling's shapeless form quivered, and it let out an agonized shriek.

"Again!" The brownies had Gristle by the hair and were trying again to pull him free.

Hadley raised her hand over it.

"Let him go," she growled. "Or I'll flash you again."

She had no way of knowing if the creature would understand, or care. But it writhed and slithered off her friend.

"Kill it!" The brownies let go of Gristle's hair and stood in front of the darkling, spears raised. "It would've done as much to us!"

She stared at the dark spot, the living shadow that had tried to kill her friend. Their kind would've surely killed them all, just made them drift off into a dreamless sleep from which they wouldn't wake up. She glanced over at the others still pinned to the ground and struggling against the nails. If she killed this one, she'd have to kill the others too. Leaving them pinned to the ground seemed cruel.

Instead, she leaned down and pulled the nail out of the ground. Untethered, she expected the creature to slide away. Instead, it pooled before her, an unshaped oil slick on the forest floor.

"I won't kill you," said Hadley. "I don't want to kill anything. I just want to find my family."

The darkling didn't move for a moment, as if considering options, then it slid across the ground toward the other two, still pinned to the ground.

Family...

The darkling's windy voice had no emotion, no sense of urgency, but she understood its meaning. Before the brownies could protest, she walked to the darklings and pulled the nails from out of them.

The three creatures congealed into one massive black pool in front of her, then moved back toward the trees outside the firelight.

"What'd you do that for?" The brownie poked her shoe with his spear. "Now they'll go get reinforcements!"

"And they'll be back for us when we sleep," said the other brownie. "Letting them go was a tactical error."

"Maybe," said Hadley. "But it was the right thing to do."

She turned and hurried to where Gristle still lay on the ground. Wherever the darklings had touched his skin, purple marks appeared as if the creatures were sucking his life through his skin.

The brownies crawled over his body and leaned near to his mouth.

"Will he be alright?" She knelt beside him but kept her distance so as not to be in the brownies' way.

"Who's to say?" The larger of the two pressed his ear to Gristle's chest. "I don't think he's dead."

As if in response, Gristle farted, then he shifted and gave a loud snore.

"He's fine," said the other brownie. "Darklings put you to sleep to feed off you. If you can't get them off, you never wake up. But it was only on him for a moment or two. He should wake up presently."

"Is there anything we can do?"

"Just wait," said the smaller brownie. "He'll come to when it's time."

"Until then," she said. "What do I call you two?"

The brownies looked at each other with confused expressions and then back to Hadley.

"Why should you call us anything?" The larger brownie sounded almost offended while the smaller one brandished his spear at her.

"No," said Hadley. "I mean, what are your names?"

"Oh," said the smaller one. "I'm..." He let out a shrill tweet followed by clicks and chirps that sounded like crickets.

"And you may call me..." The larger browner launched into a series of tweets with a slight buzzing noise and a few grunts included for good measure.

Hadley stared for a moment. There was no way she could repeat the sounds they'd made. In fact, she wasn't even sure how they'd made the sounds in the first place.

"I can't say that," she said.

"Of course you can't," said the smaller one. "You're *people.*"

"Do you have any *people* names?"

"Why would we?" said the larger Brownie. "Not like us to go fraternizing with your kind."

"Then how do you speak my language?"

"We're taught it from an early age," said the smaller of the two. "In case we come into contact with people."

"Well, I've got to call you something," said Hadley. "I can't just keep calling you 'brownie,' can I?"

"Why not?"

"It's rude," she said. "I call my friends by name."

"We're not friends," said the larger of the two.

"Then why'd you help us?"

"Chief told us to keep an eye on you," said the smaller one. "He didn't know you knew magic. Said to keep you out of trouble."

"That makes you friends," she said. "And friends need names. Since I can't pronounce yours, I'll call you Tom." She gestured to the larger. "And you, Jerry," she said to the smaller one. "Is that okay?"

Tom and Jerry shrugged at each other.

"Fine by us," said Tom.

"Now," she said. "About Gristle..."

"Nothing to be done," said Tom. "He'll wake up when he does."

"Unless he doesn't," said Jerry. "Then..."

"Quiet, you," said Tom. "Point is, best now for you to get some rest. We'll stand watch."

Hadley was about to protest when her head spun and she lost her footing. She sat hard on a log by the fire.

"Yeah," said Tom. "Lots of power you threw. Need to rest now."

It was like Grandma said. There was a consequence for everything. The power had to come from somewhere. In the heat of the moment, she hadn't thought to try to pull it from anything around her. She'd just used the power inside of herself. And now she could barely keep her eyes open.

She leaned against a rock and stared at the dying fire. Even though she didn't think it possible, she drifted into a deep sleep.

CHAPTER FOURTEEN

H adley awoke with a start. Beneath her back was the hard ground instead of her soft bed, and darkness pressed in around her except for the dim glow of the campfire. For a moment, it seemed everything that had happened had been a dream, but her surroundings confirmed it to all be reality.

She leaned against a rock and stared into the dying fire. It was a long time before morning, she supposed, and she was exhausted, but there was no way she would be able to go back to sleep. Not after everything that had happened. Brownies, puckwudgies, darklings, changelings—the woods held so many creatures that were supposed to be made up, only legend. And yet brownies stood watch in the trees. A puckwudgie snored at the edge of the fire ring, rendered so by darklings, and a changeling had her brothers and her grandmother, who, it turned out, was a witch. In fact, she came from a family of witches, and magic was something her whole family knew. Did her mother know about the other creatures? The changeling took her sister, but what about the others? How could she not? And if she knew, why did she never tell?

The logs in the fire spit with sap and crackled as they collapsed into themselves. A chill crept across her skin.

"You should be sleeping."

Hadley jumped at the voice. She looked down to see Jerry on the ground next to her.

"I was," she said. "I woke up. I don't think I can go back to sleep."

"Try," he said. "You won't be any help to your brothers if you're too tired to fight the changeling."

"I don't know how to fight."

"How did you expect to get them back, then? Ask nicely?"

She hadn't considered the how yet. When she left, all she knew was she needed to get to them. But what she was going to if she found them was another matter.

When, not if.

"But you've got magic," said Jerry. "You made the light. You must have some way to fight it."

"I've never fought anyone," she said. "With or without magic. Much less a changeling. Can she be beaten?"

"I don't know," said Jerry. "She's old. Older than the trees, even. I don't know if something that old can be beaten."

"What do you know about her?"

"Only what others have told me," he said. "They say she can't die, that she controls the woods, and that her lair is littered with the bones of people and folk alike who tried to beat her."

The hairs on her arms stood against the dread in her belly.

"I thought, maybe, with your magic, you might have a chance," said Jerry. "But now, I don't know."

"Then why are you here?"

"Orders," he said with a proud chin-thrust. "Besides, there's no love between the folk and a changeling. She used to live on her own territory, but then she started taking ours. Said we only lived here by her grace and generosity. When the brownies fought back, she slaughtered half of us. Not many of us folk left anymore."

"He's worse off than we are." Tom stepped out of the shadows on her other side and pointed to Gristle with his spear. "I don't remember the last time I saw another of his kind in these woods. Time was, there was a village of them not far from here. But now, it's like it never existed."

She couldn't imagine what it was like to lose not only his family but also his entire species. It was little wonder he was angry, little wonder he had a hard time trusting.

"Sleep," said Tom. "At least try. We'll keep watch. First light, we'll wake you and be on our way."

He stepped back into the trees and became one with the shadows.

Hadley slid Grandma's book back into her backpack and then pushed it under her head to use as a pillow. It was hard and had rough corners, but it was better than the rocks or the cold dirt. As she lay down, she turned her eyes skyward. Instead of stars, all she saw were the skeletal fingers of tree branches overhead, and she wished, not for the first time, that she'd never come to Grandma's house.

If she'd stayed home, she would never have learned that magic was real, would never have learned how to use it. But she'd also be blissfully unaware that things like changelings and darklings and puckwudgies and brownies were real. She was perfectly happy before she knew they were, so she imagined she would've been happily ignorant the rest of her life.

More, if Mom had let her stay home, the boys wouldn't have been taken. Grandma would still be in her house and not the victim of a changeling. And if she'd have stayed home, she wouldn't have broken the rules. She wouldn't have gone into the woods, wouldn't have let Patricia into the house. Everyone would still be safe.

"This is my fault," she said softly. Jerry turned his head toward her.

"I did this. It's my fault they're gone."

"You didn't create the changeling," said the brownie. "You didn't tell her to take your nan or your brothers. Whatever you may have done, that much at least is off your shoulders. Now sleep."

With the warmth of the fading fire at her back, Hadley closed her eyes and drifted back into a fitful sleep.

When she opened her eyes again, the fire was long cold. The chilly air nipped at her legs and blew the hairs on her arms rigid. She rolled to her side and looked for Tom or Jerry. Tom stood on a rock a few feet away, his tiny brow creased.

"What's wrong?"

"See for yourself." Tom gestured toward the woods.

At first, she didn't understand, as the haze of sleep clouded her perception. But the rocks weren't where she remembered them. The vague path they followed was gone, and trees she didn't recognize, twisted and gnarled, surrounded them.

"How?"

"The changeling," said Tom. "She controls the trees. She knows you're coming, so she's making it difficult for you."

A momentary pang of hopelessness hit her, but then she remembered Grandma's trick with the string and the nail. It didn't matter how the trees rearranged themselves, the simple spell would work. It had to.

She hurried over to Gristle's sleeping form and shook him.

"Wake up," she said. "We need you."

"Darklings," mumbled Gristle, his tongue heavy with sleep. "Where? What?" He shook his head and struggled to sit up.

"The darklings got you," said Hadley. "If it hadn't been for the brownies—"

"Brownies?" His eyelids snapped open. "Where? Why, I'll kick them over the trees, I will! You watch if I don't!"

"They saved us," she said. "If it weren't for them, we'd both be dead."

Gristle's expression of fury shifted to one of suspicion.

"Saved us, did they? Where're they at?"

Tom and Jerry both appeared from behind Hadley's ankles, spears at the ready and proud.

"You two saved us?" They nodded. "And why'd you do that?"

"Orders," barked Tom. "Our king commanded we keep you safe."

"And what's he want in return?" He leaned down and squinted at them. "Something pricey, I reckon."

"In return," said Jerry. "He wants you to kill the changeling. Even if we and the puckwudgie and the others don't survive, he wants us to help you get close enough to the changeling to kill it."

"Others?" A pit opened in Hadley's stomach.

"Your brothers," said Tom. "And your grandmother. Even if the beast kills them, you must keep your promise to kill the creature, else you let the roots take you."

"No," said Gristle. "You don't put that kind'o burden on a child."

"They're my family," said Hadley. "I'm going after them whether you like it or not."

"She'll kill you," said Gristle. "An' worse. She'll play her games with your mind. Drive you mad. Make you see who you most want to see, then make them do the deed."

"Is that what she did to you?"

It was a cruel thing to say, foolish and thoughtless. The old puckwudgie's face turned ashen, his eyes round in shock. Then, the hair of his beard bristled and his eyes hardened.

"What she done to me, girl, you won't never know. What she done to me was worse'n anything you've ever experienced."

His voice grew louder as he shouted.

"You don't know what it's like to have your family just gone, then to see them doing the kinds of things that haunt your dreams. She looked like my wife. Like my little'uns. Like my mam and pap. When she came for me, I ran. I hid. And that's why I'm still alive and they're not. Cause I'm a damned coward. Better she'd have killed me too."

Hadley sat stunned. No matter what she said, nothing could've made up for dragging the memories back into the light. The shame of it weighed heavy on her shoulders. The possibility of the changeling looking like something else had occurred to her, but that it could look like her brothers or her grandma never had. A creature of such abilities that would do such things couldn't be anything but pure evil in her mind.

"You run along home now," said Gristle. "I'm going to find her, and if I can, I'll take payment for my family out of her hide. If not, let her take me so I can rot and see them again."

"But my brothers—"

"They're gone," said Gristle. "You want truth? There it is. Move on with your life."

Her heart pounded in her ears and behind her eyes. They weren't gone. They couldn't be. She and her brothers didn't always get along, but the thought of life without them was too horrible to consider. And what would happen to Grandma? Would she become a ghost like Grandpa, or would the changeling take even that from her? And without her, what would happen to Grandpa? Or Mom?

The more she thought about it, the hotter her anger grew until it roared inside of her.

"You don't get to tell me what to do," she shouted. "Just because I'm *people* doesn't mean I can't help! I'm bigger than all of you! And I've got just as much reason to be here as any of you!"

"I just meant—"

"You're being selfish and stupid," she said. "I can help. It's my fight, too!"

She slammed her hand down onto a rock. At her touch, a sound like thunder erupted from her fingertips, and the rock split into a thousand pieces. Tiny bits of gravel flew through the air. The force of the blow knocked her down and sent Gristle over on his backside.

After a moment, he slowly got to his feet. Tom and Jerry appeared beside her and glared at Gristle. For a moment, they seemed ready to attack.

"Aye," he panted. "You might just have a chance after all. What about you two?" Gristle eyed them with a dour expression. "You coming, too?"

"We go where she does," said Tom.

"We're under orders," said Jerry cheerily.

"Fine," said Gristle after a moment. "Let's all of us just go marching to die. Only, in case you've not noticed, the woods've shifted again. I got no clue where we are."

"I have a plan for that." Hadley raised the nail on a string from her pocket.

CHAPTER FIFTEEN

The nail urged them forward until they came to what appeared to be a field covered with shrubs as high as Hadley's chin. She stopped and stared and then looked from right to left. As far as she could see, a stark line marked where she stood and where the bushes began. The nail pointed to the other side, so it was clear. If they wanted to get where they needed to go, the way was through.

"I'm walking ahead," said Gristle. "You can't see nothing with them *people* eyes. And the bushes are too thick. But maybe I can see under them. See what's coming. Maybe something bad. Keep the brownies above the leaves."

She nodded. Jerry, who rode atop Gristle's head, leaped to Hadley's outstretched hand. She placed him on the opposite shoulder as Tom.

Gristle raised his bow and stepped into the thicket. As the branches closed over his head, he disappeared from sight.

"Gristle?"

His bow jutted from the leaves.

"Here," he said. "Follow close."

Easy for him to say. If he turned around, he could at least see her feet. But puckwudgies seemed to be made to blend with their surroundings. That, coupled with the fact that he was short enough that the shrubs covered him completely, made following him next to impossible. She relied on Tom and Jerry calling directions in her ears to keep up.

The further in they walked, the thicker the bushes grew, until it became difficult to take a single step in any direction.

"I think we're stuck." Gristle's voice came from somewhere close by, but she still couldn't see him.

"Maybe we should go—OW!" Pain lanced through her leg as if someone had poked her with a hot needle.

"What's that? Are you—OUCH!"

The shrubs rustled where Gristle stood.

"By the roots," he shouted. "I'm tangled up! OUCH! When did these—OW! When did they grow thorns?"

Another stab at her legs drew Hadley's eyes downward. Through the leaves, branches moved past her legs like snakes.

"That's not possible," she said under her breath.

"Look!" Tom pointed across the field where a ripple moved through the brush. As she watched, the brambles tightened and formed a solid front against them.

"They're alive!" shouted Gristle. "We has to go back!"

"No!" Hadley looked behind, but the living brambles had closed ranks behind them and turned the field into a sea of wicked points and writhing leaves. She couldn't go back even if she wanted to, which she didn't. Going back meant giving up on her family. The only way out was through.

"Fight!" she shouted. "We have to get through!"

She pulled her backpack off and swung it hard in front of her, clearing a few of the branches with its bulk. But for every one she swept aside, three slithered in front of her, each covered in thorns that seemed thirsty for blood.

Tom and Jerry leaped from branch to branch, their tiny spears flashing, but their two spears were useless against the millions of thorns.

"Help me!" screamed Jerry as he parried a line of brambles. Hadley reached to pluck him out of harm's way when one branch he hadn't seen reared up behind him like a scorpion's tail. Before she could call out a warning, the thorn flashed and stabbed him through the middle.

He didn't scream, didn't even cry out. His face didn't twist in agony but wore a mask of confusion. He gasped and then looked down to see the tip of the thorn protruding from his belly, then he fell off the branch where he stood. His tiny body didn't even raise the dust when he hit the ground below.

"No!" Tom's spear flashed as he dove through the tightening branches toward the ground. He disappeared from sight.

"There's too many!" Gristle's voice came from beneath the canopy, followed by an agonized cry. She could only imagine the damage the thorns were doing to his tiny body.

If only she had the strength to throw fire to burn them all. But if she did, Gristle and Tom and Jerry—if he was still alive—would burn too. And where would she even get the power anyway?

An idea flickered in her mind. Grandma had said that to use magic, the power had to come from somewhere. She also said she could use the energy from the things around her. Maybe she didn't need to use her own energies to destroy the brambles.

Hadley closed her eyes and tried to ignore the thorns that ripped at the flesh of her legs. In her mind's eye, she saw the energy that animated the shrubs, gave them life and let them wriggle around like snakes. Then, she pictured the well of power inside herself, the roiling energy at her core.

Instead of letting it pour out, however, she imagined it sucking inward like a whirlpool. She spread her arms wide and pictured the power flowing into her like electricity.

The limbs by her legs quivered and froze and then turned black and crumbled to ash as the life force that gave them motion flowed out and left them husks. As the power flowed into her, Hadley's heart beat faster, her hands shook, and it felt like every hair on her body stood at attention. It was working. She pulled harder.

The flood of energy into her body made her muscles spasm and her jaw clench. She couldn't close her eyes, no matter how hard she tried. Everywhere she looked, the black ash that had been the living brambles reached out from her like a plague. It had worked, she'd saved them, but it was too much. Her arms and legs felt like they were on fire. Her heart pounded like it would beat its way out of her chest. She wanted to scream, but she could only take short shallow breaths.

Gristle stood from the ashes and shook himself and then ran to her side.

"What'd you do?" he shouted. "You damned fool girl, what'd you do?"

"Tom," she stammered. "Jerry."

"You can't keep it all in you like that," cried Gristle. "You'll burn yourself out! You gotta let it go!"

She heard him, and on some level she understood, but knowing what he wanted her to do didn't mean she knew how to do it. She'd sucked in too much power, like lightning through a single copper wire. As her limbs tightened and her heart pounded, all she could think of was a wire burning through.

"Let it go!"

She threw her head back, closed her eyes, and screamed. Heat from her core seared out of her, burning her lips and scorching her tongue.

"Not all at once!" shouted Gristle. "You'll burn!"

Without Grandma to guide her, she had no way to know how to control the flow of magic. But she had an idea. Mom had an old lamp in their house, one that had a dial on it. For bright light, one needed only to turn the dial all the way up. To dim the lights, one needed to turn the dial down. She pictured the dial in her mind, attached it to the flow of power that was rushing out of her, then slowly turned the dial down.

The heat that rushed out of her slowed until her lips were warm instead of burning, then she sank to the dirt and coughed on the stench of burnt hair.

"Tom," she said again. "Jerry."

"Here, Miss." It was Tom, caked in ash. In his arms, Jerry lay.

"Is he..?"

"Alive," said Gristle. "But hurt something fierce. Needs a healer, he does. That's a right nasty hole in his middle."

"Had worse," coughed Jerry, though it was obvious it was more bravado than anything else.

Tom trilled at Jerry in a voice that sounded like mournful crickets. When Jerry chirped back, it stuttered in a way that tugged at Hadley's heart.

"We need to get help," she said.

"Didn't your nan teach you nothing about healing magic?"

The herbs Grandma taught her were for headaches and fever, sour stomachs and burns. Nothing about how to heal someone who'd been impaled through the middle.

"Please, Miss," said Tom. His eyes glistened with tiny tears. "If you can, please help him. Anything. Just don't let the roots take him."

She didn't know what he meant, but it wasn't the time to ask. She sat in the ash and pulled Grandma's book from her backpack. Maybe there was something that could help, but she didn't know how to ask for it. It wasn't like a sprain or a cut. It was far worse.

She raised her hand over the book and concentrated on the aged pages, then she pictured Jerry's injury in her mind.

To say it out loud would be too terrible a thing, so she called it silently.

Mortal wound.

The pages stirred then fanned deep into the tome. When they came to rest, there was a drawing of a person on the ground, his life draining away as mourners watched. At his side, a person knelt with hands raised above. Below the image, only a single line was written.

To save the life of another, you must give a bit of yours.

The meaning was obvious. She could give some of her own power to infuse Jerry and could possibly save his life. However, she didn't know how. Was the power of a brownie the same as the power that coursed through her body? And how much? The power of the living brambles still made her skin tingle, and the pain of drawing in too much was still fresh in her mind. She could only imagine what too much power would do to a creature so tiny. Still, she had to try.

She knelt and held out her hand to Tom, who gently laid Jerry in her palm.

If she could pull energy in by picturing what she wanted it to do in her mind, maybe she could direct it by doing the same. It was just a question of the right images in her head, she reasoned. She closed her eyes and focused on the miniscule weight of Jerry in her hand, then she pictured the power inside of her flowing down her arm and pooling in her palm. As she did, her hand grew warm, and Jerry let out a soft whimper.

"Careful, now," said Gristle. "He ain't but a tiny thing."

Hadley extended a finger on her other hand and pointed to the hole in Jerry's midsection. She knew nothing of brownie anatomy, had no way of knowing what got punctured or how serious the wound was, so instead of picturing things knitting together, she whispered the only thing she could think to say.

"Be well."

From her finger came a trickle of power, an eyedropper full at most. When it was done, Jerry opened his eyes.

"I feel warm, ...," he said. "It don't hurt no more."

He smiled, but even so, the wound in his abdomen didn't close. He needed real help from a real healer. At best, she could prolong his life, make him comfortable.

"You rest now," she said. "We'll look after you."

"Stupid." Tom's voice broke as he fought back tears. "Should'a seen that thorn coming. What'm I going to do without you in my life?"

"I'm fine," said Jerry. "Really, I am. A little rest and I'll be right as rain."

Tom looked from Gristle to Hadley and then back to his fallen friend.

"We need to carry him," said Hadley. "Somewhere he can rest where he won't be in danger."

"If I may, Miss," said Tom.

Before she could answer, he darted up her arm and into her hair. It took him only moments, but when he was done there was what amounted to a nest made of her blonde locks, perfect size for a brownie, hanging just below her ear.

"Here," said Tom. "You just rest here. See? I hung it close so you can still help out with advice. You're a smart one, you are."

"Oh," said Jerry. "Must be grim, if you're calling me smart."

"Shut up," said Tom, though he smiled when he said it.

Hadley lay on the ground so Jerry could be eased into his cradle, then she stood slowly so as not to jostle him. When she'd reached her full height, she looked about. His weight felt secure in her hair, not like it could unbalance or fall out.

"Okay," said Jerry. "But I'm only resting for a little while. I can still help."

"Of course," said Hadley. "What is your king's name?"

Jerry tweeted with the call of a jay, punctuated with a crow's caw.

"He'll know of your bravery," she said. "And you can tell him yourself when you're all healed up."

"That'll be nice," he said, then he closed his eyes and slept.

CHAPTER SIXTEEN

*O*nce upon a time, there was a little girl in the woods...

Mom used to tell her stories at bedtime, and many of them started the same way. A girl in the woods met strange creatures on her way to have an adventure. And when Mom told the stories, they always had a happy ending. The evil thing was defeated, the strange creatures earned their reward, and everyone lived happily ever after.

But Mom's stories never talked about little girls having their legs ripped up by brambles. They never talked about the real trauma the strange creatures went through that made their journeys so perilous. And in Mom's stories, none of the creatures ever suffered a thorn through the belly, or if they did, they were healed by magic. Her magic wasn't good enough, and whether he felt better or not, she couldn't escape the notion that the brownie in her hair was dying.

The nail spun and pointed, and she glanced to her companions. The puckwudgie kept sharp eyes ahead, his bow in his hand, an arrow nocked. Tom the brownie rode on Gristle's shoulder, spear raised. It was just like one of Mom's adventures. But despite the familiar beginnings, she couldn't help the sinking feeling that there weren't to be any happy endings. Not for any of them.

"How is this taking so long?" It wasn't a question for anyone in particular. "The woods just aren't that big."

"Changeling magic," said Gristle. "The woods ain't that big, but it fools you into thinking it is. The trees and paths move and lead you in circles."

"But the nail is supposed to lead us the right way."

"Yes," he said. "But only if your mind is clear. Is it?"

They stepped through the tree line to a familiar site.

"I guess it isn't," she said.

In front of her was Grandma's house. Or rather, it looked like Grandma's house. But there was something about it that wasn't right. She couldn't point to any particular thing as wrong, but something about the house just wasn't exactly as she remembered it.

"We've gone in a circle!" Gristle groaned. "All this time, and you've been concentrating on the wrong place!"

"But I haven't," she said.

As they stepped closer, the wrong of the place became more apparent. Instead of clapboard and stone, the "house" was made up of trees woven together as an imitation, an imperfect reproduction of Grandma's house. The corners bent and twisted just a bit so that, from a distance, the house seemed to lean. But the closer she got, the more she realized that the doors were made from thick shrubs, the roof from branches.

"Are we supposed to go inside?"

"I don't want to," said Tom. "But I will if you do, Miss."

"I'm ready for a challenge," said Jerry. He waved his spear and then fell back into his hammock.

"Changeling magic," said Gristle. "She takes what's in your head and uses it to twist your mind."

"Do you think she's in there?" Hadley's skin prickled beneath the heavy shirt.

"Ain't nothing in there but death," said Gristle.

"Then we go around," said Hadley.

"I doubt it will be that simple," said Tom. "With a changeling, nothing is ever simple."

Hadley turned to go back the way they came but was greeted by a wall of tree trunks and leaves. She turned back toward the strange house. If she couldn't go back, the most logical course of action was to try to go around. But trees and branches slithered around the house like snakes, wound around one another, and formed a barrier she couldn't hope to pass. As tight as the trees wrapped twisted and turned, even the brownies wouldn't be able to pass.

"Looks like we have to go through," said Hadley.

Gristle grunted in response and then took a few tentative steps forward.

"Don't trust nothing you see in there," he said. "Just like that looks like your Grandma's house but ain't, there's bound to be stuff in there what looks like things you know but ain't. Don't let it take you off guard."

Hadley nodded and then took a few tentative steps into the yard. When she was a few feet away from the tree line, the sound of creaking wood and rustling branches made her spin. Around the yard, the trees and shrubs became a wooden solid version of the veil. They were in, it seemed, and the only way out was through.

She nodded to Gristle and then walked toward the house. Wherever she stepped, there were imperfect reproductions of Grandma's yard, but she kept her eyes on the front door. Grandma's door was dark red with brass fittings, and it creaked when it opened. The door in front of her was similar, but the red looked more like blood and the golden color of the knob was due to the wood from which it was made. It made her wonder if it would make a sound when it opened and if it would be a creak or a scream.

They climbed the steps to the wide porch and stepped to the door. With a sideways glance, Hadley reached for the doorknob and pushed. The door swung wide without a sound, which she found more disturbing than if it had let out some imperfect groan or creak.

"Remember," said Gristle. "Both of you. Don't trust nothing."

Tom squared his shoulders and held his spear at the ready from within the tangles of Gristle's beard. Hadley reached for her hair and felt to make sure Jerry was still where he should've been, then she took a deep breath and stepped across the threshold.

As with the outside, the inside looked familiar but somehow wrong. Everything was *where* it should've been, where she remembered it being, but nothing was *what* it should've been. The couch in the living room was made of rocks and shrubs, the curtains of vines that hung from branches. From somewhere deep within the house, someone sang a curious wordless tune.

"Is that her?" whispered Hadley.

"Likely not," said Gristle. "Not like a changeling to show itself so quickly."

Something in the voice struck a familiar chord, just like the rest of the house. It was something she knew, something she ought to recognize, but it was somehow imperfect. It took her the space of a few breaths for her to realize who it was supposed to be, another breath for a stone to form in her gut.

"Grandma?"

She took a step toward the stairs.

"It ain't your grandma," said Gristle. "Don't trust it!"

But the voice was so nearly hers, as if filtered through cotton. And the song, so nearly the one she seemed to have always known, since her Grandma had been singing to her since the day she was born. If it wasn't Grandma, then who was it?

From above, heavy footsteps ran across the upper floor, and the voice that might have belonged to Grandma screamed. With Gristle's warning in her ears, she ran for the stairs.

"Grandma!"

Hadley took the stairs two at a time until she reached the landing on the second floor. Like everywhere else, it looked more or less as she remembered it, but imperfect. The forbidden doors to the bedrooms were closed, but they were slightly wrong in shape, in color, in height or width.

More footsteps on the stairs. The person who may have been Grandma screamed again, and Hadley ran to catch up. As she rounded the corner onto the second flight, she glimpsed a foot in a white slipper as it was dragged out of sight. She dashed up the stairs until she stood on the third floor, as imperfect a reproduction as the rest of the house.

There were three closed doors. At Grandma's house, one led to her room, one to the room the twins shared, and one to the restroom.

"We need to leave." Gristle's voice wavered behind her. She turned and found fear written over his hairy face. Though his eyes were bright and large and his bow was drawn, there was no sense of the bravado he usually had. He was afraid, and there was no point in denying it or putting on airs.

"We can't," she said. "Grandma—"

"That thing ain't your grandma," he roared. "That thing's going to get us all killed—or worse. We should leave before it's too late."

Hadley...

Her name came without a voice but seemed to be a product of the house breathing. The walls around her swelled and contracted, as did the doors to the rooms and the floor on which she stood. From behind the door to her left, the one that in the real world went to the room the twins shared, came a low moan. After a moment, it was joined by another in terrifying harmony, then something slammed against the other side of the door.

Hadley!

Two moans, louder than before, came from behind the door as the things in the room hit it again. The moans increased in volume, raising in pitch until they became terrible screams. In the back of her mind, an image formed of what was behind the door, what hit it faster and faster to try to get to her, but she didn't want to give the thought voice.

Wood splintered, and the door burst forward, broken off its hinges, and landed on the floor. What stood before her was more or less what she envisioned, but imperfect in the execution. The faces resembled her brothers, only twisted with rage and hunger. But they sloped at the waist until there was only one pair of legs. The twins. She'd thought of them as one entity before, owing to their peculiar habit of always being near one another. But she'd never said as much to anyone. The nightmarish vision stood in the doorway, four arms swinging and flexing, the heads biting at one another.

Hadley, run!

The voice in her head, the muffled Grandma voice, came as Gristle launched arrows at the thing. Tom leaped from his post, spear raised, and attacked the creature. Each head bellowed, then it stepped out of its room, brushed the brownie to the floor, and came toward her. Her brothers' faces snarled and snapped.

She made to move toward the stairs, but the creature lunged in front of her, blocking her path. The only place she could go was the mirror house's version of her room.

As Gristle fired the last of his arrows, Hadley grabbed him by his bushy beard and threw herself at the door. It swung open freely. Tom hurried through after him, then she turned and closed the door as quickly as she could and pushed the privacy deadbolt into place. On the other side, the creature pounded and roared.

"What is that thing?" Gristle held his bow like a club.

"My brothers," said Hadley. "It's like everything in the house is the same as Grandma's, but wrong."

Gristle lowered his bow.

"Them's your brothers?"

"Not my real brothers," shouted Hadley. "They're like this place. Everything's wrong, somehow."

The door cracked and a splinter fell away. The creature stared in through the broken door.

"Quick!" Tom leaped to a chair. "What do you remember about your room?"

Hadley turned to look. There were plenty of similarities. The canopy bed, the chair, the vanity, even the door to the balcony was as she remembered. The only differences were in the construction and the proportions.

"I don't know," she wailed. "It's just a room!"

"If it's in your head," said Jerry from his hammock, "it'll be in this room. She built it from your memories. What can you use?"

"What's that door?" Tom pointed to the French doors on the wall.

"My balcony," she said. "I read out there."

"How high up?" Tom stroked his chin for a moment.

"Third story," she said. Then, as the thought of his plan hit her, the door exploded inward. The creature snarled as it scanned the room until both sets of eyes fell on her. Hadley ran to the doors and threw them open. Beyond was the balcony, but instead of it standing over a moonlit yard, her reading spot seemed to be suspended in the center of the galaxy. The sky was awash in purples and greens, blues and yellows. Below, the grass was nowhere to be seen, replaced by an endless sea of stars.

Her heart pounded as she turned and faced her brothers. If they caught her, she didn't have much of a chance. But more, if they caught her, her real brothers and Grandma wouldn't stand any chance at all.

The creature took slow, deliberate steps toward her and stalked her onto the balcony. Over its shoulder, Gristle and Tom stood ready to pounce. All she had to do was get it to come a little closer and then avoid four arms that wanted to tear her to pieces.

"Boys," she said. Her voice shook, though she tried to sound authoritative. "You're not allowed in my room. I'll tell Grandma."

The creature paused for only a moment, then the heads looked at each other and laughed. If she needed any proof that the nightmare in front of her wasn't her brothers, the laugh let her know. The boys seldom laughed, and when they did, it was a sweet sound. The creature brayed like a mule when it laughed, obnoxious and devoid of the self-conscious hesitation that marked whatever it was that made the boys different.

"I mean it," she yelled. "Get out! Or I'm telling Mom!"

Both heads bellowed and it ran at her, arms wide. When it came so close it couldn't possibly stop, she dropped to the floor and shot between the creature's legs. At the same time, Gristle and Tom attacked. While the brownie stabbed at its leg with his spear, Gristle hit the creature in the back with his shoulder, sending it over the rail and into the starry beyond. The creature's faces twisted in surprise and then fear as realization set in. It grasped for the rail, but too late. Hadley ran to watch it tumble end over end as it fell and faded into nothingness.

"We have to leave," said Gristle. "The changeling ain't in the house, you can bet. This place was set up to wind us up, keep us playing her game for a bit."

"But I heard—"

"You heard what she *wanted* you to hear!"

Maybe, but she doubted it. Maybe the singing, maybe the voice from above, but what about the voice in her head? What about Grandma's voice that told her to run? Surely the changeling wouldn't be so clever as that, would she?

"What else is on this floor in the real house?"

"Why does that matter?"

"It matters," said Gristle. "Because she's pulling the images from your memories. If something exists in your memories, something like it exists here."

"This is just my room," said Hadley. "My brothers' room is where that thing came from."

"Anything special in your room?"

"No," she said.

"Then we need—"

Before he could finish his statement, another noise echoed through the house. Though she couldn't place it, the shrill sound struck her at the base of her spine and set her legs to moving. All she wanted to do was get away from it, to run and hide before whatever made the sound found her.

Jerry clutched a blanket of hair while Tom leaped from Gristle's shoulder and raised his quivering spear toward the stairwell.

Hadley, run!

Grandma's voice exploded in her mind, along with the image of the four of them outside the house and in the back yard. The meaning was clear, that they had to escape. The thing below them seemed far away but closing in fast. She hit the stairs going downward at a run. At the second floor, the sound was a physical blow that sent her teetering backward toward the stairs.

"What is that sound?" Hadley clamped her hands over her ears, but it did nothing to block out the noise.

"Who else was in the house?"

"No one," she said. "No one except...

The figure that emerged from the stairwell was not her grandfather, any more than the house in which they stood was her Grandma's house. But, like the nightmarish version of her brothers, the thing that stood in front of them was imperfect, exaggerated almost to the point of being unrecognizable. It had Grandpa's flannel tablecloth shirt, his white beard, and his mud-stained work boots. But there was no trace of the kindness in Grandpa's smile. The face was torn and distorted by rot, and empty holes were all that remained of the Grandpa's kind eyes. In his chest, a gaping hole revealed a dark cavern where his heart should've been.

"Where're you going, sweetie?" The voice was Grandpa's if Grandpa had spent years buried in dirt and sand. "Ain't you going to introduce your little friends?"

She screamed as the creature reached for her. Gristle grabbed her by the waist and threw her backward, away from its grasp.

"Find us a way out!" He swung his bow like a club at the thing's head. The impact was palpable, but it didn't stop coming.

For a moment, she couldn't move. But Jerry tugged her hair and shouted in her ear, and it was enough to break the horrific spell.

Like in Grandma's house, there were doors on the second floor. She ran to the first and tried the knob, but it wouldn't turn. It was less an actual knob and more just a knot that had grown in the house. The second door was the same. When she came to the third, the knob turned and the door swung wide.

"In here," she shouted. Tom darted ahead of her while Gristle gave the Grandpa creature a fierce shove, sending it toppling down the stairs. He ran into the room and slammed the door behind him.

"What took so long?" he grunted as he dragged what appeared to be a dresser in front of the door. "Couldn't you get the other doors open?"

"This was the only room I went in," she said. "It didn't have anything to build them off of, so I guess they're just doors that don't open."

"Makes sense," he said. "What was so special about this room that you had to get in?"

"Nothing," she said. "It was unlocked. The others weren't. Grandma said not to go into the locked rooms, but she must've forgotten to lock this one."

"And?" Gristle stared at her. "Did you find anything? Was it worth snooping?"

"It was my mother's room," she said. "From when she was a little girl. I found her diary where she talked about her sister, Patricia, who died."

"So that's who she looks like now, eh?"

"I guess so."

"Anything useful?"

"No," she said. "I wasn't in here for that long."

"Over here!" Jerry waved his arms from a windowsill. "There's no glass. We can hack away the branches and climb down."

The doorframe shook as a massive weight slammed into it.

"Hadley! What're you doing in that room, young lady!"

"Go," shouted Gristle. "Hurry!"

Tom used his tiny spear to chip away at the vines that made up the window while Hadley pulled with her hands. Gristle braced his back against the dresser and pushed to hold the door closed, but every time the Grandpa creature slammed into it, it opened just a little bit further.

"You'll never get out!" The ruined face leered through a crack in the door. "And even if you do, you'll never find them! Never!"

The vines in the window gave way, and Hadley peered out into the void. Just like what lay beyond her reading spot, the only thing below the house seemed to be an ocean of stars.

"Out!" Gristle strained against the door.

"There's nothing out there," she cried. "I can't jump into nothing!

"Ain't none of it real," shouted the puckwudgie. "Don't jump, climb!"

Without any further instruction, Tom scrambled through the window and disappeared from sight. Hadley tried to steady her breath, but between the pounding of her heart and the Grandpa creature's struggle to get through the door, it was all she could do to get a good grip on the windowsill with hands that shook. As she lowered herself through the window, the sounds of splintering wood echoed through the darkness. Half a second later, Gristle vaulted the sill and swung down next to her onto the side of the house.

"Get a move on," he shouted as he scurried downward. "That thing's madder'n a nest of wet hornets!"

Hadley glanced up in time to see the rotten face of the Grandpa creature jut through the window, then a paw made of rancid meat swiped out the window at her. She ducked and hurried downward.

"Hadley!" it screamed. "Come back here! They're mine now! Mine!"

It ducked back into the house. Hadley froze to the vine, certain that a huge shoe would come over the side as the Grandpa creature chased them down to wherever they were headed. When it didn't come, she couldn't bring herself to feel relief. She couldn't trust it.

They climbed for a long while, too long to be down the side of a simple three-story house. Her arms burned with fatigue and her lungs felt like they would explode. Every time she gripped a vine, she found it harder and harder to close her fingers around it.

"Gristle," she called. "Where are we?"

"Don't know." His voice sounded far away, too far to be just below her. "Can't see the ground."

"Tom?" No answer came.

"He can't have gone far, Miss." Jerry's voice in her ear at once startled and soothed her. No matter how far the others had gone, Jerry was at least by her side.

"How're you feeling?"

"Tired, Miss," he said. "Although, I reckon I should be terrified. I just can't seem to conjure the feeling."

She didn't like the sound of that.

"Do you have any pain?"

"No, Miss," he said. "Just tired."

"If we ever get to the ground, I need to check your wound."

"How do you mean, Miss?"

She looked down.

"I feel like I've been climbing forever, and I still can't see the ground."

"But it's right there, Miss," said Jerry. "I can see it as plain as I can see your ear."

Hadley looked down, but below there was no grass, no forest floor. Below her were only stars in a dark purple sky.

"Where?"

"Just below your feet," said Jerry. "Just there. Can't you see it?"

She couldn't. In fact, when she looked down, her stomach roiled at the sight. Letting go of the vine wall surely meant tumbling off into the vacuum of space. She'd heard blood boiled in space, that lungs exploded. She'd heard she'd freeze to death in the icy grip of the nothing beyond.

Hadley.

Her name floated to her from across the void.

Let go.

It wasn't the Grandma voice she heard. It was Gristle's. But it couldn't be. Gristle was below her, too far to be seen. The voice sounded like it was right below, maybe at her ankles. He'd said to trust nothing, and it was a warning she took to heart. Especially if whatever it was wanted her to let go.

Let go, Miss!

Another voice. This one was unmistakably supposed to be Tom, but there was a peculiar quality to it, like he was speaking from inside an old soup can.

Her fingers ached and bled, scratched and busted open from the rough wooden vines that made up the side of the house. Every time she tried to find another grip, it was like dragging her tiny hands through gravel. Still, she couldn't give up. Her brothers and Grandma were counting on her.

As she adjusted her hands and lowered herself down a little more, something snaked around her ankle and grabbed tight.

I got you!

She screamed and held on, though muscles in her hands and joints in her fingers burned.

We got you, Miss!

Hadley looped her arm around a thick vine hugged it tight, tears streaming down her cheeks as she chanced a look downward. The thing around her ankle was a vine like the ones that made up the rest of the house. But this one took the shape of an old, gnarled hand.

"No," she screamed. "Stop! Let me go!"

You have to let go! The voice was more insistent. *We've got you!*

She kicked her feet and screamed, all the while holding onto the thick vine as hard as she could.

What's gotten into her?

She don't know it's us.

The changeling was trying to trick her, that was what it was. Gristle told her not to trust anything she saw or heard, and it was solid advice. The changeling could use anything against her, and it proved it with the nightmare versions of her family. There was no way she was going to fall for another lie.

Damned people *eyes can't see nothing the way it really is!*

She paused. People eyes? It sounded like Gristle. But couldn't the changeling sound like him too? Couldn't it sound like all of them?

"I can see the ground," said Jerry. "It's just below us. Tom's down there too."

Hadley stopped fighting. If Jerry was right, she could let go and get away from the house. But if he was wrong, if the changeling had him fooled as well, letting go would send her to die. It came down to trust. She couldn't trust herself, so she had to decide if she could trust her new friends. She closed her eyes, took a deep breath, and let go.

For just a moment, she hung weightless while her stomach fluttered, then came the whoosh of air as she toppled backward. Then, her feet hit solid ground and she rolled onto her back. The deep purple universe blotted away into clear blue sky framed with trees, and Gristle and Tom looked down at her.

"You alright?"

She sat up and looked around. The house was still there, but the branches and vines that made up its walls shriveled as she watched, the leaves on its roof turned brittle and fell apart. As the whole thing turned to mulch, she felt a nervous giggle bubble in her belly.

"I couldn't see the ground," she said. "I could hear you, but I thought it was the changeling."

"How'd you figure out it was us?" Tom leaned on his spear.

"Jerry," she said. "And then, Gristle, you said something about people eyes, and, well, I just trusted."

"Dangerous," said Gristle. "Can't trust nothing. But glad you did."

Hadley knelt and lowered her head so Tom could get a look at Jerry in her hair. Even though she couldn't see the brownies from her vantage point, Jerry's ragged breathing told her all she needed to know.

"He's no worse off, Miss," said Tom. "But he's no better neither. He needs a healer. Bad."

"We should go back," said Gristle. "Take 'em back to their own kind. Maybe one o' them knows how to heal him."

"We can't," said Tom. "We're under orders. We go back, we've deserted our posts. There'll be no healing for him. They won't even let us back into the village."

"Grandma could do it," said Hadley. "She knows more healing herbs and spells than me. We just have to hope he can hang on until we find her."

Chapter Seventeen

Gristle walked ahead, his bow out in front of him. He had no more arrows, so the best he could hope to do was swing it like a club. Still, he didn't let it stop him.

Tom rode on her shoulder next to Jerry, who slept in her hair still. Every now and again, he made little sounds like crickets or cicadas, sounds she was certain was either him whispering encouragement or even singing to his partner. It tugged at her heart, the way he spoke to his fallen friend. But it also made her feel good for Jerry, that he had someone like Tom in his life. It made her more determined than ever to find Grandma and the twins.

Hadley stopped. Gristle stood at a fork in the path and looked from one way to the other. Then, he turned to her.

"I don't know where we are," he said. "Forest is all changed, all turned around. We could be right back where we started or we could be in another world for all I know."

She fished in her pocket and pulled out the nail on thread. Just like before, she concentrated on Grandma, on the boys, on finding the creature that wore Patricia's face. But the nail didn't point toward either path. Instead, it wavered from one side to the next then back again.

"Fat lot of help that is," said Gristle. "Now what do we do?"

"CHOOSE!"

The voice came from above, shrill and harsh. Hadley looked up toward the voice and saw a large black bird with icy blue eyes staring down at them.

"It's a damned crow," said Gristle. "They's in her service. What they see, she knows."

"Where's my family?" She stamped her foot and shouted, as if a bird in a tree cared at all what a silly girl demanded.

"CHOOSE!" it said again. "CHOOSE!"

"Let me, Miss," said Tom. He cocked his spear back.

"No," said Hadley. "Don't kill it. She wants us to play her game? Fine. We'll play. But I want my family back!"

She turned, and without a thought, she took the left-hand path, Gristle close behind. As her foot touched the path, a cold wind howled past and chilled her deep in her bones, then came the rustling noise she knew too well. When she turned back, the opening to the path was gone, closed in by a wall of trees and shrubs.

"Well," said Gristle. "Now you done it. We're stuck here."

"You couldn't have done any better," she said. "This path was just as good as the other. Come on."

She raised the nail and concentrated. This time, the direction was clear, straight down the path. She rolled it up and stuck it back in her pocket. Nothing left to do but get on with it and see where the path led.

The path turned from grass and dirt to gravel and black rocks. The further they walked, the darker it seemed to be. The trees of the forest, so lush and green, here lost their leaves and reached skeletal fingers to the sky. The wind carried the smell of damp rot, and she wondered, not for the first time, why she didn't just obey the rules.

"Miss," said a tiny voice in her ear. "I think it's getting colder."

In truth, it was getting hotter by the second, but Jerry's body burned with fever.

"We have to stop," said Hadley. "He's getting worse."

"How will stopping help him?" Gristle crossed his arms and scowled through his beard.

"Maybe I can help him," she said. "I don't know. I have to try."

She leaned down to let Tom take his partner from the hair hammock and lay him on the ground next to the road.

Jerry's face was slick with sweat, and his olive skin was a pale shade of green.

"He don't look good, Miss," said Tom. "You got to help him if you can."

She didn't dare try to pour more power into him. She didn't know how much he could take or even what a second infusion would do. If only she could ask Grandma for advice.

But, in a way, she could. She pulled the book from her backpack and set it on the ground, then she held her hand over it and closed her eyes.

"Fever," she said.

At her command, the book flew open and pages fanned by. Where last time there was hesitation from the grimoire, it obeyed her without question this time.

The pages stopped on an entry about medicinal herbs. She read as quickly as she could and then turned to Gristle.

"These trees," she said. "What are they?"

"Lotsa different kinds," he said. "Ain't never just one kind."

"Do you know what a Black Elder looks like?"

"Sure," said Gristle. "Why?"

"I need the flowers off it," she said. "And the berries as well. Can you find them?"

"Don't know what good it'll do," he said. "He's done for."

"Don't you say that!" Tom leaped to his feet, spear in hand. "He' ain't done for! He ain't!"

"All I'm saying is—"

"You shut up, puckwudgie," screamed the brownie. "You shut your hairy hole and go find the Miss what she needs, or so help me, I'll—"

Gristle raised his hands in surrender and then hurried off into the woods.

"Thank you," said Hadley.

"Anything to help him," said Tom as he stared at Jerry. "He just can't leave me. We're a pair, he and me."

"Then I'll need your help too," she said. "I need water. Just a thimbleful, but it's necessary. Can you find some?"

"I will, Miss," he said. "Don't know where, but I will."

He darted into the underbrush and was gone.

The book said that a tea needed to be made of Black Elder blossoms, and that would bring the fever down. The berries, on the other hand, were to be crushed and prepared and pressed into the wound to draw out any infection. Which meant she needed kindling for a fire. She scooped Jerry up and gently guided him back into the hair hammock, then she took a few tentative steps into the woods to find twigs.

"It must be nice," she said. "having someone like Tom. He's so brave, but even more so when it comes to you."

She didn't expect Jerry to answer. In fact, his shallow breaths were all she could hear from him. But it felt good to talk out loud, more normal and less like she was alone in the woods.

Twigs were in no short supply, and it took her no time to gather a few handfuls from the forest floor. She made her way back to the road and decided any spot was as good as another, then she put the twigs in a pile. Another brief bit of concentration and the twigs smoked and burst into flames. As they did, the trees around her screamed.

"She burns us!"

"Fire!"

"Murderer!"

From around her, old and wooden voices shouted and cried out as branches shook and limbs flailed. The trunks of the ancient black trees twisted until the knotholes were eyes and the patterns in the bark were mouths. Their voices came like squeaking wood and cracking timber.

"Stamp it out! Stamp it out!"

Several limbs thrashed in their boughs and rained down upon her tiny fire until it was driven into the dirt and put out, then the limbs creaked and came for her like wooden snakes.

As the prickly branches closed around her body, she screamed.

"Let her go!" Gristle's voice cut through the din. The puckwudgie sprinted onto the path and raised his arms in front of the tree that held Hadley prisoner. He gently lowered his bow to the ground and then bowed.

"You travel with this one?" The tree glared, or seemed to, hard through its knothole eyes. "She broke our sacred rule. She produced fire!"

"Oh," said Gristle, his voice full of reproach. "You didn't. Tell me you didn't."

"The trees," she shouted. "The trees are alive!"

"You made fire? In these here woods?"

"I had to," she cried. "I had to make a tea for Jerry—"

"She made fire!" The tree's voice hit her like a blow to the head. "She threatened our roots and limbs!"

"By the root," said Gristle. "She didn't know, did you? Why didn't you tell me you was gonna make fire?"

"I didn't know the trees were alive!"

"All creatures are alive," boomed the tree. "And you would do well to remember it!"

Another voice came from the other side of the road, where Tom hung suspended by his ankle from another tree branch.

"This one," said the tree, "We found beyond his kingdom, apart from his kind. He seeks to take our land!"

"I do not," shouted Tom as he thrashed. "I needed water."

"He admits it," said the tree. "He aims to steal our life source!"

"And why are you here, puckwudgie?"

"Lords of the forest," said Gristle in a low bow. "Blessed by the root and hugged by the soil. Please, we meant no harm. We're just passing through."

"To what end?" The tree turned its knothole eyes toward Hadley and brought her closer to its face.

"I'm trying to find the changeling," she said. "It took my family."

The branches shook and a rustling murmur passed among the leaves. As they spoke, the branch that encircled Hadley loosened and lowered her to the ground.

"It is not unknown to us," said the tree. "The oldest of our kind saw its arrival, saw the changes in the forest over the years. It is a plague, a fungus to us."

"Our friend." She moved her hair aside to show Jerry asleep. "He's dying. He needs help. Water, a fire to make tea, plants."

"You carry him though he is not your kind?" The trees rustled in conversation. "Who are you to care for folk?"

"He's my friend," she said. "Friends help friends."

The bark of the tree's face creaked as it shifted into a thoughtful expression, then its trunk shifted. The others let Tom gently to the ground.

"We will help," said the tree. "You will have what you need."

"But the fire..." She didn't want to endanger them, but Grandma's book said the herb had to be taken as a tea.

"Rocks," said Gristle. "You can't just go building a fire anywheres. You gotta build a fire ring so it can't escape and hurt 'em."

Together, they gathered stones from the sides of the path, from the bases of trees, from wherever they found them. When they'd claimed enough, they put them together in a circle. With every twig placed into the circle, Hadley tried to show her reverence for the sacrifice being made to help her friend. She tried to imagine what it was like, to see pieces of her used as fuel. After all, the twigs were dead wood, but they were still once part of the forest.

When the fire was set, one of the trees dipped a branch low and released several very large leaves, which Gristle wove together into something that resembled a bowl. It wouldn't last long, but she hoped it would last long enough to steep the tea.

When the bowl was finished, another tree lowered its branches. Dew, living water, dripped from its leaves. She gathered enough to fill the bowl. All that was missing was the herb.

"I couldn't find no Black Elder," said Gristle. "I heard you screaming before I found one."

The tree branches rustled again.

"Why do you seek the Black Elder?" The tree's woody voice was full of suspicion.

"The blossoms and berries," said Hadley. "They are what makes the medicine for my friend."

"Then we are truly sorry," said the tree. "There is but one Black Elder left in these woods, and it has borne neither blossom nor fruit for a very long time."

"Hasn't," said Gristle. "But can it still?"

"We do not know," said the old tree. "The Black Elder is older than all of us, and it keeps its own secrets. Only it knows the answer."

"Where?" said Hadley. "Show me. I have to try."

"But you must go alone," said the tree. "The Black Elder is a solitary tree. It will not take kindly to an audience."

"What do I say?"

"We shall instruct you on how to address one so old with respect."

The trees around her were silent as she walked across the leaf-covered ground. Wherever she looked, she expected them to talk, to move, to turn knotty faces toward her, but they didn't. They slept, their leafless branches scraping the sky with skeletal fingers.

The Black Elder stood deep in the forest, said the old tree by the path. Finding it wouldn't be a problem, nor would knowing it when she saw it. According to the tree, it would be unmistakable.

Hadley followed the directions the tree gave her until she came to a small rise in the land. At the top, she looked down at what had to be the Black Elder.

In her mind, she'd pictured a tree like any other, maybe darker, maybe older. What stood at the center of the clearing was unlike any tree she'd ever seen. True to its name, the Elder's obsidian bark seemed to be made up of shining coal. Its immense trunk twisted at the base, which was larger than even Grandma's house. Great roots dug into the ground like snakes at its base, which was littered with the bones of hundreds of small animals.

She slowly crossed the distance toward the tree.

"Great Lord of the Forest," she said as she knelt. The old tree had told her what to say, and she'd repeated it until she could say it without faltering. "Blessed in root and soil, please hear me."

Though neither the tree nor branches moved, the air filled with the sounds of dead dry leaves rustling.

"Leave us," it said. "Let us rot."

"Please," she said. "I need to talk to you."

"We are tired," said the dry voice. "We are dying."

The roots that went into the ground, big as elephant trunks and bigger, were covered in lichen and moss in places. In others, grey fungus crept up the bark. She followed its progression until she found a large patch of the grey on the side of the tree, taller than a house, wider than she was tall.

"What did this to you?"

"It came to our woods a long time ago," said the Elder. "It has taken many shapes, has been known by many names. But wherever it exists, it brings only ruin."

"The changeling," she said.

Low rumbling shook the ground as the Elder's trunk untwisted to reveal a vast pattern of knots and holes. To her mind, they formed an ancient face.

"What do you know of this creature?"

Her stomach knotted under its gaze as her first instinct was to duck her head, hide her eyes, run, and cower from the massive tree. But she stiffened her spine and thrust her chin forward. To command a tree's respect, the tree by the path told her, one must present a proud trunk.

"The changeling took my brothers," she said. "And my Grandmother. I'm trying to get them back."

"Your grandmother…" The Elder's bark features softened. "We know her. We remember her. She respects the old ways."

"Yes," said Hadley. "She does. And I love her. Very much. Please, help me get her back."

"What do you ask of us?"

"My friend," she said. "A brownie. He was hurt very badly. We need your blossoms and berries to heal him."

"Then," said the Elder. "He will die."

"No," said Hadley. "He can't."

"All things die, child. All things return to the soil to feed the root to rise up again. It is the way of the world."

"But…" What could she say to a thing such as a tree to make it feel what she felt? A thing so old it had seen the cycle of life over and over couldn't possibly have the sense of what it meant to hold the life of one so small dear. To it, the brownies' lives, even her own life, must've been fleeting.

"We no longer offer our berries or blossoms," it said. "The rot and disease that came with the changeling has corrupted them, poisoned them. We cannot help you."

"Are there others like you? Maybe—"

"We are the last of our kind in these woods," said the Elder. "Once, our kind held prominence. No longer. We are all that is left."

"I'm so sorry," said Hadley.

"It is as it must be," said the Elder. "All things born must die. All things that live must return to the soil."

Around her, the bones of small animals seemed testament to the fact. Squirrels, rabbits, fox, all lay about the roots of the Elder.

"What killed all of these creatures?"

"We did," said the Elder. "To prolong our life. They came too close, as you did, so we devoured their lives."

Dread bathed her insides in ice.

"Are you going to do the same to me?"

"We might have," said the Elder. "Once. But we are tired now. We no longer care to live. We are content to die and to let the forest die with us."

"But..." The thought was too horrible to comprehend. Even among dark twisted trees plagued with disease and rot, for the entire forest around Grandma's house to be gone was a thought she couldn't bear. "You can't. You just... can't."

"We do not answer to you," the Elder whispered. "You know nothing of our existence. We knew the land when the forest was young. We watched the rise and fall of the folk, watched the arrival of people, and marked the passing of both. It is time for us to end."

"Please," said Hadley. "Let me help you. Let me try."

Grandma's book said that healing could be done through a transfer of power. Pushing a little power into Jerry had prolonged his life thus far. She had no reason to believe it wouldn't work also for a tree. The trouble was, the Elder was much bigger. She doubted she would have enough power if there were ten of her, much less only one.

Around her, there seemed to be nothing to draw power from. The grass was brown and dead, and what other trees there were showed signs of even more decay and fungus. The only power source she had was herself. It seemed hopeless. Regardless, she placed a hand beside the fungus patch on the Elder's trunk and closed her eyes.

The river of power that flowed from her core swirled and churned, a vortex of raw energy. In her mind's eye, she directed it just as she had with Jerry, made it flow up her body and down her arm, into her hand, and over the diseased portion of the Elder.

The fungus shivered and convulsed then began to move. But instead of moving off the tree or drying up, it grew. It moved like a slug over the obsidian bark of the Elder and then attached itself to her fingers and began a slow climb up her arm.

"There," said the Elder. "You see? You, like so many others came to help. But it feeds on life. It feeds on warmth and power. It will suck you dry, then it will come back to us."

Hadley jumped backward, flailing her arm as she moved. The fungus wouldn't come off, though. It held fast and continued its climb up her arm. Wherever it touched, it left a bloody trail, and the higher it went, the weaker she grew.

"Please," she cried. "I only wanted to help! Please!"

"It is the way of things," said the Elder. "Everything born dies. Everything that lives above the soil returns to the soil."

She thrashed and screamed, trying to scrape the fungus off her arm, but when she pulled, her flesh tore as well.

It was brought by the changeling, the Elder said so. The changeling was folk. There had to be something she could use against it that wouldn't hurt the tree. Salt maybe, but she'd left her backpack with Gristle. The only thing she had was...

"Iron!"

The idea hit her at once. Iron affected folk. It hurt the darklings. Maybe the fungus was made of similar stuff.

She pulled the iron key from around her neck and held it against the advancing infection on her other arm.

It sizzled and twitched and then retreated from the key's touch. Wherever she touched it, it retreated from her skin but left bloody tracks in its wake. She used the key to push it off her, then waved the key across the side of the Elder. The fungus retreated and inched its way off and onto the ground. When it was completely off the tree, Hadley put the key on top of the spoor and watched as it smoked and then burst into orange flame. She stood between the Elder and the fire until all that remained was a smoldering pile of ash.

There was more of the fungus on the tree, higher than she could reach. Removing all of it would take more time than she could spare, but she removed as much as she could as high as she could reach. When she'd finished, she stepped back to appraise her work.

The fungus left scars behind, deep chasms in the already rutted surface of the tree. It made the Elder look like it had been through a battle.

The Elder's knotholes shifted and grew.

"We feel better," it said. "How have you done this thing when all of the folk who tried could not?"

"Iron," said Hadley. "Folk can't touch it, but I'm not folk."

"Remove the rest," said the Elder. "Heal us."

"I can't," said Hadley. "I can't reach the rest, and there's too much. There's no time. My friend is dying, and if you can't help me, I want to be there for him and his partner when he dies."

The Black Elder shuddered and then its creaking voice grunted as a branch lowered. When it was at Hadley's eye level, it stopped and shook. As she watched, blossoms formed.

"Take them," said the Elder. "And use their power to heal."

The branch shook and the blossoms fell away into Hadley's hands. Then the places where the blossoms were swelled into red berries.

"Pick them," said the Elder. "Use them as you will. But you must make us a promise. You must return. You must make us whole again."

"I will," said Hadley. "I promise. When I find my family, I'll come back."

Her reply seemed to satisfy the old tree, and its trunk twisted back around so the knotholes were no longer visible. Hadley took her prizes and ran back the way she'd come.

CHAPTER EIGHTEEN

Jerry stirred. His fever broke almost immediately after he'd drunk the tea made from the Black Elder's blossoms. The berries, ground into a paste, were spread over his wounds and they no longer smelled of rot. His eyes flickered open.

It was the first time Hadley had taken a really good look at the brownie, though she'd been traveling with him for some time. His eyes were the color of clean pennies and shone as brightly.

He chirped a weak cricket sound, which Tom echoed with a smile on his face and tears in his eyes.

"He asks if he's still alive," said Tom.

"How does he feel?"

Jerry grinned and then clicked and chirped.

"Hungry!" Tom whooped. "He's hungry! He wants food!"

"Means he's better," said Gristle. "Good. Now we can get moving."

"This path," said the tree. "Leads to darkness. You would be wise to turn back now, accept your losses, and be grateful for the lives you still have."

"What?" Hadley stared at the old tree. "No! We can't! We've come so far already—"

"The changeling does not care," said the tree. "She will not give your family back. She will corrupt you, as she has these woods, and watch you die."

"Don't care," said Gristle. "She's done too much. Been here too long. Someone's gotta stand up to her. Changeling already took what was mine. I'm not going to let it take all of hers too."

"Then," said the tree, "we shall give you food for your journey and mark your passing when it comes."

From the branches above fell apples, oranges, peaches, pecans, and other fruits and nuts that Hadley liked.

"Take your fill," said the tree. "And be on your way. May your return to the soil be peaceful, and may you nourish the root."

It was, to Hadley's mind, a nice way of saying "we hope you'll die fast and painless," and that they'd eat their bodies when they were dead.

"We thank you," said Gristle in his most formal manner. "And we'll be on our way."

Hadley ate a peach and a few walnuts, and she began to feel better. But with the hunger pangs gone, her attention was drawn back to the situation at hand. Less than a week ago, magic was make-believe, brownies were folklore, and she'd never even heard of a puckwudgie. Yet one walked in front of her with a brownie on its head. Another brownie still hung in her hair, and magic was something she was learning to use. In her world before, trees were for climbing or cutting down, not things that talked and offered morbid blessings.

The path was still lined with trees that reached up and formed a canopy overhead. Could they talk too? And if so, why weren't they saying anything?

"What's that nail of yours say?" Gristle didn't turn to face her but kept his grey eyes forward on the path.

"Straight on," said Hadley. The nail hadn't turned against the path in ages.

"What I thought," he said. "We've been here before."

The thought struck her as silly.

"How? We haven't turned or anything. "We've been following this trail."

"Yeah," said Gristle. "Tricky, changelings are. Especially
this one."

He took his bow and rubbed it against a rock beside the
row, leaving a long red mark. When he was satisfied, he
gestured for Hadley to follow him. Another minute or two
of walking, he stopped and pointed.

There was a rock beside the road, one that looked like
the other one, with a long red mark on it.

"That can't be," said Hadley. "We passed it."

"Aye," said Gristle. "But remember what I told you
about changelings? They's good at illusion. You think
these woods is really this big? It's had us walking in circles
for a while now."

"What does it mean?"

"Means we's getting close," said Gristle. "Trouble is, we
could walk right past it and never know."

"Wait," said Hadley. She knelt on the path and took off
her backpack, then she pulled Grandma's book from inside. Maybe there was something inside, something about
how to see past the changeling's deception.

She put the book down, held her hand over it, and concentrated.

"How can I see what's real?"

The book shuddered then flipped open. Pages fanned past until it stopped on a page with a single phrase written on it.

"Open your eyes," it said.

"That's no help," said Gristle.

It didn't make sense. Everything the book had said before was helpful. Beside the phrase was an illustration of a face, one that looked an awful lot like Mom, holding something up in front of her eyes. Recognition dawned on her as she reached into her pocket and pulled out the river stone she'd taken from her mother's room.

"It's a witch's stone," said Gristle. "Where'd you get it?"

"It was my mother's," said Hadley. "I found it in her room."

"They're rare," said Tom. "Only made when the water of a river manages to cut its way through solid rock."

Hadley closed one eye, held the stone up to the other, then looked through.

The difference was stark, as it appeared she was looking at an entirely different landscape. The dark skeletal trees were, through the witch's stone, green and normal, without a face among them. The path, littered with debris and black sand, was a trail through the woods, overgrown and green. Further down, the cemetery Patricia had shown her lay just off the trail.

"It's this way," she said as she took the lead.

Hadley stepped into the cemetery with reverence. If creatures like puckwudgies and brownies were real, if trees could talk and magic was alive, maybe every other story she'd heard was true too. Grandpa was a ghost, another impossibility until she came to Grandma's house. Maybe the dead in the cemetery could hear her.

"What're we doing here?" Gristle's head twitched back and forth like a bird's as he looked for danger. "I doesn't like cemeteries."

"I want to see something," said Hadley. "I want to know why the changeling kept me from coming here."

"I'll stay with you, Miss," said Jerry from his hammock in her hair. "You needn't be afraid. I'll keep a sharp eye out."

She couldn't decide if he was trying to be funny or brave, but she decided on the latter.

"Thank you," she said.

Through the witch's stone, the cemetery looked like any other she'd been to, only smaller. Since she knew what it was and knew what it looked like, she decided to chance it and see if she still needed the stone. When she took it away, nothing changed. The small stone wall still marked the borders of the graveyard, dead leaves still carpeted the place. She tucked the stone back in her pocket.

The cemetery in Austin where Daddy was buried was huge. His grave was small and used a simple headstone to mark where he lay. When she stood in front of it, everywhere she looked were more headstones in neat rows. This one was smaller, though. There were only two headstones in the ground, with four more leaning against a tree. Four open graves sat next to the other two.

The first stone was for Patricia, the *real* Patricia, who died when she was a little girl. The second was Grandpa's. Hadley's stomach churned as she hurried to the tree where the headstones leaned. As she read the names, a sob stuck in her throat.

One was Grandma's. One was for each of the twins. The last one bore her name.

"It don't mean nothing," said Gristle. "The changeling's messing with your head, that's all."

But as she moved to leave the graveyard, she chanced a look into one of the open graves.

At the bottom, Hadley saw herself in a wooden casket, dressed in white linen. The Hadley in the grave's hands were crossed over her chest, her hair in braids. Hadley froze on the spot and stared.

"It's me," she said, a scream rising from her gut. "I'm dead. It's me."

"It ain't you," shouted Gristle. "Don't look at it! Don't think on it. The changeling's messing with your mind."

Before she could tear herself away from the sight of herself in death, the corpse's eyes snapped open. Instead of the pale blue of Hadley's eyes, the dead Hadley's eyes shone green. It sat up and let out a feral snarl as it leaped and dug its fingers into the walls of the grave. It was climbing. It wanted to get her.

"It ain't real!" Gristle held his bow like a club. "It's all in your mind, girl! You've gotta shut it down!"

The corpse version of Hadley gained inches toward the surface, and it rotted with the seconds. As it pulled, its teeth turned black, its skin sallow. Then the skin grew taut, its hair thin, and the scream that came from it sounded choked with dirt. Hadley tried to back away from the sight of her dead self-consumed with decay in front of her but stumbled and fell backward onto the ground.

From the other three graves, more sounds came, hollow and mournful cries that struck at Hadley's nerves. There were dead versions of her family in those holes, and they were coming out to get her.

"What do we do?" she cried.

"Run!" Gristle took her by the arm and dragged her to her feet, back to the trail. Tom clung to the thick fur on his back while Jerry shouted incomprehensible tweets and sounds in her ear. Behind them, the dead versions of her family emerged from the graveyard and followed.

Up ahead, the trail widened to a spot Hadley was sure she recognized. The little shack, Patricia's treasure hoard, stood just a few yards away.

"In there," she shouted.

She pushed her legs faster than she thought they could go, but somehow Gristle, whose legs were shorter, was still faster. Only when they came to the door of the hoard did she chance a look behind them. The dead were still coming, closer than she thought. She gave the door a hard shove and dove inside. Once Gristle was in, she pushed the door shut and put her shoulder to it.

For a moment, they held the door, eyes closed, teeth clenched. But then they listened and heard nothing. There were no running footsteps, no howls of fury. The only sounds were their own labored breaths and the sounds of their own hearts in their ears.

"Where are we?" panted Gristle.

"We're here," said Hadley. "This is where Patricia keeps her treasures. This is where she'll be."

PART THREE

DOWN THE THROAT, INTO THE BELLY

Come out to play, if you feel brave,
For now the time is right.
Darkness swallows up your soul,
and toothy shadows bite.
From *Bedtime Story,* by Scott A. Johnson

CHAPTER NINETEEN

N o one moved or even made a sound. For a moment, Hadley was afraid to back away from the door, so certain the ghouls of her family would burst through and eat them. But the silence stretched like a yawn in the darkness of the shed until, eventually, she realized they were safe. Either safe or exactly where Patricia wanted them, which was anything but.

"What's this place?" Tom jumped down from Gristle's back and kicked at the floor.

"Patricia's hoard," said Hadley. "It's all stuff she's found. She brings it back here and keeps it like buried treasure."

"Huh," said Gristle. "It didn't seem this big from the outside."

It was true. The outside looked barely the size of a garden shed, but Patricia's treasures sat heaped in piles against the walls. It shouldn't have fit, but it did.

"Well?" Gristle looked at the walls and ceiling. "We're here. Now what?"

She didn't know. The farthest she'd thought was to find the shack. To her, it seemed to be the only place Patricia could be. But she knew so little of the changeling, so little of the woods. As she looked about the small space, it struck her how absurd the idea was. The changeling could be hiding anywhere, could look like anything. Why would it want to live in a shack full of garbage in the woods?

"She's not here," said Hadley. She sank to her knees as the reality struck her. After they'd come so far, with darklings and trees and living brambles, after Jerry had almost lost his life, there was nothing. They fought their way to the trove for nothing. Her lip trembled, and she tried not to cry, but the thought of her lost brothers, her grandmother, dragged a sorrowful moan from her. She rubbed her hands across her tear-streaked face and pulled at her hair, as if to do so would wipe away whatever veil kept them hidden.

"Maybe," said Gristle. "Maybe there's more to this place than meets the eye."

A sob stuck in her throat as a new thought struck her. She fished into her pocket and withdrew the witch's stone and held it up to her eye. For a moment, she just stared, then a grin crept across her face as her sobs turned to jerking tears of joy.

"It's not what it seems," she cried. "It's not a shack at all!"

To the eyes of the folk, and to her unassisted people eyes, the dirt floor was strewn with toys and trinkets, a blanket, and bones. The walls were bare pressed wood with barely enough substance to keep out the wind, much less ghouls and monsters.

But through the witch's stone, everything became clear. They stood, not inside a shack, but just inside the mouth of a cave. The treasures were real enough, though there were more of them. Against the stone walls stood piles of baubles and trinkets, and it became clear they were more than just things Patricia had found in the woods. They were spoils, things taken from the other folk that lived peacefully in the woods until she came along.

"Looks like a shack to me," said Tom. He banged on one of the wooden walls, which sounded real enough under his tiny fist.

"But it's not," she said. "Look through the witch's stone."

She lowered it to Tom's face, and he looked through, but his expression didn't change.

"Still looks like a shack to me," he said.

"Gimme that," said Gristle. He held the witch's stone to one of his eyes and closed the other. "Don't look no different to me. Must be something about your people eyes. Maybe there's something in that book of yours."

"I tried," she said as she took the stone back. "All it said was 'open your eyes.' That's no help."

"What'd you ask it?"

"How can I see the truth," she said.

"You asked it wrong," said Gristle. "Ask it something else."

"Like what?"

"You're the witch," he said. "I don't know how magic works."

Neither did she. Not really. He called her a witch, but she was less than a novice. Grandma had only just begun, only scratched the surface of what true magic was. She could start fires, yes, and make light, but there was so much more she didn't know.

The only thing she did know was that she had to try. Her brothers needed her. Grandma needed her.

She sat cross-legged on the shack floor and took the book out of her backpack and gently placed it in front of her. With her hand raised over it, she closed her eyes.

"How can I break the illusion?"

The book shuddered then pages fanned. When they stopped, it was on a different page than before, one with more than one phrase written on it. An illustration of a woman, arms spread and toes pointed, showed light pouring off her.

"Burn away shadow lies with light," she read. But she was already so tired, she wasn't sure if she had enough energy left to manifest a light so bright, even if she could figure out how.

"I can't," she said, a sinking feeling pooling in her gut.

"You can see the way," said Jerry. "Just lead us."

It was worth a try, and stranger things proved to be true. She took Gristle by the hand and let Tom climb to her shoulder, then she raised the witch's stone to her eye and walked. When she came to where the wall of the shack would be, she continued walking. Gristle and Tom, however, fell backward. Her hair pulled as Jerry's hammock stayed at the edge of the wall as well.

"We can't," said Gristle. "Can't see it proper, and it keeps us out."

There was no way around it. She either had to leave her friends behind or use more of the precious energy she had inside.

"Miss," came Jerry's voice from her ear. "If need be, you can take mine. It ain't much, but you gave me what you had when I needed it, and I'd like to return the favor."

"You'll die," she said.

"Might," said Jerry. "Don't know. But if it helps you get your family back, I'm willing."

"But I'm not," she said.

She rummaged in her backpack. Surely, there were a few more apples, some nuts, any of the food given to them by the trees. But after a few moments, she realized they'd not carried much and had eaten what they'd carried.

There was nothing left to do. Whatever the consequence, she needed to try the spell.

"Take him," said Hadley as she took Jerry from his hair hammock and placed him on the ground. "And keep back. I don't want anyone else getting hurt by mistake."

Gristle scooped up the brownies and took as many cautious steps backward needed until his back was against the shack's door. Then, Hadley read the page in the book, put it down, and spread her hands wide.

There were no magic words to say, no wands to wave. It was a simple matter as she understood it. Simply picture what she wanted to happen, then make it happen. Obey the natural law, visualize the power flowing from her center, then push it out.

The room slowly brightened, then the light from Hadley's middle intensified. Wherever it touched, the illusion faded and left the truth behind. But it wasn't strong enough. Not yet. She had to push harder.

In her mind's eye, the trickle of energy became a river, then a flood. As it flowed out of her body, the light at her center grew dimmer by degrees.

In the shack, the light from her center touched the walls, the ceiling, the floor, and burned away the illusion. Pressed wood and nails became creviced rock and moss. The ceiling disappeared into blackness that stretched upward, as did the wall Hadley faced. Instead of the back of the shack, a long corridor stretched into darkness.

She smiled as the spell worked, then her legs wobbled. The flood of light stopped, and she fell to the floor surrounded by velvet black. Her eyes grew heavy, but if she slept, there was no way of knowing if she would wake up.

"Gristle," she said in the pitch. "Tom."

Her voice was tiny in her ears, barely a whisper, but even so it echoed around her.

"We're here." Gristle's voice rebounded off the rock. "Can't see nothing."

"Then let's fix that." The second voice was one she knew, one she dreaded. A click, a finger snap, echoed through the chamber, and there stood Patricia.

She wore the same white linen she always wore, the same placid smile.

"You came to play," she said. "That makes me so happy."

"Where's my family?" She tried to sound forceful, but she was too tired, too weak.

"That's not how the game is played," she said. "You've been playing well so far. But let's see if you can beat me."

"Changeling!" Gristle stood, bow in hand, beside Hadley, his eyes blazing. "You're a blight! You give this child back what you stole for her or—"

"Or what?" Patricia laughed. "What can such a creature as you do to one such as me?"

Gristle clenched his jaw and stamped his feet but said nothing.

"You want to play too? Fine. Come and find me."

She disappeared, but even so, the cave stayed lit. In every crevice, every hole, luminous moss glowed blue. Hadley could see again, but all she wanted to do was sleep.

"C'mon," said Gristle. "Get up. Can't stay here."

"So... tired," she said. She could barely keep her head up and her eyes open. "Need to sleep."

"She used too much," said Tom. "She's got no energy left."

Gristle's arm disappeared into his fur and came out with an apple. It was tiny, small enough that even his hand could close around it, but it was something.

"Here," said Gristle. "You need to eat. This'll help."

She took it with limp arms and barely enough strength in her hands to hold it, but the first bite was sweet, and the juice splashed across her tongue. As she chewed the first bite into pulp, her hands felt stronger, her mind more clear. She took another bite, then another, until all that was left of the apple was seeds and the core. Then, she sat upright.

"You better?" Gristle held his hand out to her.

"Better," she said as he helped her up. "Not great yet, but better. I can go on."

"Good," said Gristle.

"Miss." Tom tugged at her sock. She looked down at him and he pointed with his spear.

Jerry stood leaning on his spear, a tired smile on his face.

"I'm with you, Miss," he said. "Proud to be of service."

"Are you sure?"

"Yes, Miss," he said. "You took care of me. First people I've ever heard of taking care of one of us folk. Makes us friends, I think."

"Of course, we're friends," she said. "What else would we be?"

He smiled, and as he did, Tom put his arm around his partner's waist.

"We'll help," said Tom. "In any way we can. Not because of orders, but because we want to."

She smiled and looked to Gristle, who stood deeper in the cave.

"I'm coming," he said. "I got accounts what need settling. Don't make no mistake about it. I want that changeling's head."

It wasn't what she'd hoped for, but it was enough.

Chapter Twenty

As they walked, Hadley's strength returned by degrees. It was good that she didn't have to expend any of her power to keep the cave lit, as the glowing moss let them see their way. Every step they took, however, brought new fear to her mind.

The changeling, Patricia, said they were playing a game. If it was a game, there had to be an object. Easy. The object was to find her grandmother and brothers. There also had to be obstacles. They'd overcome so many, what with the darklings, the living brambles, and the imperfect house with all its imperfect horrors.

But one thing Hadley knew to be true was that the closer they came to their goal, the harder the game became. That meant that whatever lay deeper in the cave was more dangerous than anything they'd faced before. Every step she took made the knot in her stomach tighten and made her heart beat just a little bit faster.

They'd not gone far, only a few minutes, before the tunnel opened up into a large cavern. The moss revealed hundreds of toothy stalactites and gave the area the feel of a giant mouth waiting to grind them to paste.

The giggling started almost as soon as they stepped inside. A dozen different voices rebounded off the stone walls until the air was full of the twittering laughter.

Gristle raised his bow like a club. Tom and Jerry both held their spears, ready to attack. Hadley reached into her backpack and grabbed the only thing she could think to use as a weapon, the bag of salt.

"What is that?" The laughter didn't sound happy or joyful. There was a bite to it, the kind that bullies used on the playground when beating up the smaller kids.

"Sounds like shriekers," said Gristle. "And if it is, don't let 'em touch you."

She'd have asked why, but movement through the rock formations caught her attention. At first, they seemed like shadows. But then their glowing blue eyes opened, and they smiled to reveal teeth like ivory bricks. Everything else about them was concealed in shadow.

"There's four of them," said Jerry. "One for each of us."

"One would be enough to do us in," said Tom. "Why so many?"

"Don't let 'em get together," said Gristle. "Scatter! Make 'em come to you!"

And do what? Hadley wanted to say. But before she could form the words, all four sets of eyes dropped from their stony perches and hunched down on the ground. Like a shot, Gristle ran for the farthest wall. Jerry and Tom gave each other a nod and a fond touch on the shoulders, then ran in opposite directions. Hadley didn't know where to run. As one of the shriekers locked eyes with her, she slowly backed away.

In the dim lighting, the thing was different than she thought. Up in the air, hidden in darkness and behind the stalactite, it seemed huge, with hunched shoulders and arms like cables. In reality, the thing was rail thin and spidery in appearance. Its long, gangly legs stayed bent at the knee, which thrust out to its sides. Its sharp elbows were similarly bent, with arms that ended in thin hands and long fingers. As the creature hunched its back, preparing to pounce, long spines stood up, which made it seem even bigger than it was.

It leaped, and as it did, Hadley threw a handful of salt at it. With the darklings, salt burned. But if it had any effect on the shrieker, it didn't let it show. It let out a cruel laugh as it landed only a few feet from her, its smile growing even wider.

Hadley took off the backpack and swung it at the creature but missed it by a foot or more.

"Don't let it touch you!" shouted Gristle. "They eat fear!"

She wanted to ask what he meant, but the creature was on the move again, slowly circling her. The salt did nothing—less than nothing. It amused the shrieker. Maybe she had something else. The iron key, the nails, the red brick dust, even Grandma's book. Something had to be proof against it.

But it was too late to reach for anything else. The creature sprang and knocked her to the hard floor of the cave. Her head bounced off the stone floor and made her feel woozy, then it was on her, the glowing blue eyes inches away, the huge white teeth so close she could see her reflection in the saliva that coated them. It bent forward and took a long sniff, up her neck and across her face, then it placed one of its spidery hands on her head. The last thing she remembered was Gristle's voice howling over the sounds of the echoing cavern.

Daddy was home. He walked into the living room in his shorts and t-shirt then sat in his chair as he always did when he put on his shoes.

"I'll be back in a minute," he said as he tied his sneakers.

But she knew. This was the day. He wouldn't be back. This was the day that someone drove too fast, someone wasn't watching.

She sat down in his lap and stopped him from tying his shoe.

"No," she said. "you can't go."

"I have to," said Daddy. "Mommy want's ice cream."

"No," said Hadley. "You need to stay here. Take your shoes off."

Daddy laughed. She always loved Daddy's laugh. He didn't laugh like he was just humoring her. When he laughed, he did it with his whole face and body, a real laugh that showed joy and love.

"Can't, pumpkin," he said. "Tell you what. When I get back, we'll do a puzzle together. How's that?"

"No!" She stamped her foot. "You can't go! There'll be an accident and you'll die! If you leave, you won't come back!"

"I'll always come back," he said. He kissed her forehead and walked out the door.

She stood on the street. Daddy was walking toward her, doing his funny fast walk when he was trying to exercise. He had his earbuds in. She could almost hear the music.

A car came from down the street. It was going too fast. She could scream. She could save him this time. But the scream caught in her throat. He saw her. He smiled and waved. Then the car hit him from behind. Daddy bent backward, hit the hood, smashed into the windshield, rolled off like a ragdoll into the ditch.

Then the scream found its way out.

She ran to where he lay in a thin pool of filthy water. Though it was dark, red swirled in the chocolate-milk brown of the water. Daddy lay bleeding, his eyes wide, his mouth crimson. She knelt by his head.

"Why?" he stammered. "Why didn't you save me?"

His head fell back and sightless eyes stared at her.

She should've stopped him, should've made him understand that he needed to stay home. She should've hidden his shoes or gone with him so he'd have to take the car or screamed and cried. But she didn't. She remembered that night the policemen in their crisp blue uniforms came to the door to tell Mom. The sound Mom made when he told her, when she slid to the floor and cried, when she screamed out and pounded against the wall. She heard it in her sleep. She should've stopped him. Mom didn't know, could never know, that it was her fault. She should have done something, anything, to keep him from leaving.

Mom turned her head toward her and glared.

"Why?" she cried. "Why didn't you do something? He wouldn't have gone if you'd stopped him! Did you want to kill your daddy? Because that's what you did! It's your fault!"

Hot tears streamed down her cheeks as her breath came in short rasps. Her throat threatened to close off as her lungs spasmed against her belly, and all she could think was that the weight of that one sentence, that single accusation, would crush her like a bug. And worse because she felt in her heart that it was true.

But it isn't.

Grandma's voice came to her again, echoed in her mind like a whisper inside a dream.

You are not to blame. You never were.

Her parents stood in front of her, Mom's face slick with tears, Dad's with blood. They stared at her accusingly, neither angry, but sad.

"Why do you think I dropped you off at Grandma's?" Mom's eyes were hot and red from crying. "I can't stand the sight of you. I left you with one simple job to do. Watch after your brothers. And you couldn't even do that."

"I'm disappointed in you," said Dad.

Don't listen. Grandma's voice whispered in her ear. *None of it's true.*

But her brothers wouldn't have gone into the woods with Patricia if Hadley hadn't invited her in. Grandma wouldn't have been taken if Hadley hadn't broken the rules. And none of them would've even come to Grandma's if Dad hadn't died.

That's not true! Grandma's voice grew to more of a wind than a whisper. *It was time for you to come! That changeling has been trying to get into our house for years. The trouble isn't your fault. It's hers. The only thing that will be your fault will be if you give up now. And even for that, I'll forgive you.*

Hadley rooted her feet to the ground and bowed her back toward the phantom images of her parents.

"You're not real," she said.

"Why did you let me die?"

"My daddy would never blame me," she said, the rage in her heart growing to a massive fire. "You're not him."

"How could you let your brothers be taken?"

"You're not my mom," she shouted. "My mother loves me!"

At her words, both apparitions shrank back, cringed even.

"Look what you've done to us," said the thing that wasn't her father.

"I didn't do anything," she said. "This isn't my fault!"

The fire inside her roared until she was sure it would burn its way out of her chest. Her anger wanted to escape, begged to burn the apparition of her parents to ash.

But it wasn't right. She couldn't. If she let it go, if she let the fire inside her out, wouldn't she get burnt, too? And when all that power was gone, would there be enough left for her to find her brothers?

She took a deep breath and closed her eyes, forcing the fire inside to calm. When she opened her eyes again, she was back in the cavern. The shrieker lay on the ground in front of her twitching. It wasn't dead, but it wasn't a threat to her anymore.

Behind her, another shrieker had Gristle by the face. His arms and legs hung limp at his sides as the strange creature lifted him off the ground and laughed. The spines on its back ruffled and undulated as it drank in whatever fears were coming from the puckwudgie, and as she watched he seemed to grow older.

Hadley ran toward the shrieker. When she came within an arm's length, she took hold of it around the neck. At its touch, her gut swam and dizziness consumed her.

Hadley fell into nothingness. There was no concept of ground or sky, no walls or dimension. There wasn't even color, save for the absence thereof, and the only thing she could call that particular nothingness was black.

Around her, images flashed, moments of fear from Gristle's life. They flitted by, birds on spastic wings, before she could see them, but every time one passed, Gristle's moans of anguish filled the air. The shrieker was digging, burrowing into Gristle's mind to find the moments of the tastiest fear, the most agonizing morsels. Gristle fought, threw up walls against it, but they all crumbled under the touch of the shrieker.

Then it came, the singular moment. The nothing faded into the interior of a hut, tiny on the inside, but only for anyone Hadley's size. For Gristle and other puckwudgies, it was perfect. Roomy, even. Their chairs had no backs but were more squat-legged stools to accommodate the anatomy of those who sat upon them. Likewise, the tables legs were shorter, lower to the ground. On it, bowls of turned wood sat full, with steam still curling up from their contents. The hearth still blazed, though the fire was dying down, and a kettle hung over it with more of the delicious-smelling food inside.

Gristle knelt on the floor, his eyes wide. The knife in his hand was almost certainly huge by his standards, but to Hadley it was barely the size of a steak knife. Red slicked the blade and dotted the dirt floor. A few feet away from him lay another puckwudgie on her back.

Hadley had no way of knowing but didn't need to be told who it was.

"It ain't Lum," he cried. "That weren't Lum."

More images flashed, of children, of screams, of moments that burned his heart until it couldn't feel anymore. But always, the image came back to Gristle with the knife, Lum on the floor.

Hadley stepped toward him. Grandma spoke to her, but she didn't know how. Could he see her? Could he hear her? She put a soft hand on his shoulder and he didn't recoil.

"It wasn't your fault," she said.

"You wouldn't know." His usual gruff voice was nowhere to be found, replaced by a soft whisper. "You weren't there."

"Tell me," she said.

"It don't matter," said Gristle. "None if it matters no more."

"Please," said Hadley. "Tell me."

"It weren't Lum," he said again. "It was that changeling. It got in her head, took her shape. It came after me. Said it was going to hurt my kids. I killed it."

"You did what you had to do," said Hadley.

"But what if I was wrong?" Gristle spun and glared at her. The red rims of his eyes showed tears, while the creases on his hairy face showed his emotional state. "What if that were Lum, and I just killed my wife? What if I made a mistake? Oh, by the root!"

He fell to his knees in a fresh round of sobs, and the shrieker purred with pleasure.

"Tell me about her," said Hadley. "Lum. What was she like?"

"Pretty thing," said Gristle. "Good cook. Smart. And she was so gentle." His chest heaved in a fresh round of sobs.

"Would she have done the things you said she did?"

"No," said Gristle. "But—"

"Were you afraid for the lives of your children?"

"I was," he said. "I swear it. It were going to hurt my little'uns."

"Then you did what was right," said Hadley. "Would Lum have done any different?"

"You don't know," said Gristle. "You didn't know her. What if I was wrong?"

It wasn't working. She couldn't distract him from his fear just by trying to talk him through it. Grandma had a gift for a soothing voice and always knew just what to say. But Hadley was loud, brash. She constantly said the wrong thing and sometimes managed to make things worse.

"They feed on fear," she said. "You can't let the shriekers feed on you."

"What shriekers?" His eyes turned back toward the body on the floor. He was lost in the moment, the single worst fear of his life.

"Gristle, don't you know me?"

"No," he said. "Go away. Leave me alone."

"But I need you," she said. "You're my friend."

"Ain't got no friends," he said. "Don't deserve none neither."

He'd slid from fear into despair, and the shrieker purred at the taste of it.

"Listen to me!" She grabbed at him, but her hands passed through his body like smoke. It made sense, after all. They weren't really there. It was all happening in his mind. She was just a shadow, a guest in the world created by his memories.

"You have to fight," she shouted. "You have to! The shriekers are killing you! You have to help me fight the changeling!"

"Changeling?" Gristles eyes snapped up toward her. "Root take it, where is that changeling? It's her fault, what I done to Lum. Where is she?"

The surge of rage that bubbled out of him made the scene in which he stood waver and fade a bit, which she hoped was a good sign. But the purring noise didn't stop. If anything, it got louder. The creatures fed on fear, but rage was fear intensified. If anything, Gristle's rage would feed the creature more and kill him faster. She had to think of something.

"Lum," she said. "She was your wife?"

"You watch how you say her name," said Gristle, a snarl on his face.

"You loved her."

"Of course, I loved her," he roared.

"Tell me about her," said Hadley. "C'mon. Tell me what she was like."

It was a risk, but one she hoped would pay off. If she could get him talking about her, his love for Lum would be more than the shrieker could eat. At least, she hoped so.

"She's dead," shouted Gristle. "Because I killed her!"

"No!" said Hadley. His mood swung again, and with it, more of his energies were being eaten by the shrieker. "You didn't! It was the changeling, right?"

"I don't know," wailed Gristle as he dissolved into a new flood of tears. "Maybe it wasn't. Maybe I killed Lum."

"Tell me about her," said Hadley again. "What was she like?"

"Gentle," said Gristle, his quiet voice full of sorrow. "Never hurt a fly, that one. Kind to everyone."

"Go on," she said.

"Good wife, good mother. She doted on our young'uns. Took care of me when I was sick or hurt, but never made me feel like a burden. But... Then she came in spitting venom. Root take me, she said such horrors. Said she hated our young'uns. Said she hated me."

"That doesn't sound like Lum," said Hadley.

"No," said Gristle, his voice pleading. "No, it don't. She said she was going to kill our young'uns, drown 'em in the well."

"Lum, *your* Lum, would never have done that."

"No," said Gristle. "She wouldn't. Not never."

"What else? Tell me more. Tell me what happened."

"She tried to carve me," he said quietly. "With this blade. Said she was going to gut me then turn it on our young'uns."

"It couldn't have been Lum, then," said Hadley.

"But she looked—"

"It was an illusion," said Hadley. "Remember? The changeling can make illusions. What happened next?"

"Lotsa folks seen what I saw," he said. "Family. Friends. Loved ones. All of them acting so bizarre. So many got killed. By the time we figured out what was happening, more than half the village was gone. Then, the changeling herself came. Not in no disguise, but her. And she burned the rest of us out."

"It wasn't Lum you killed," said Hadley. "And you have to believe that. You can't be afraid of it anymore."

"You... Your name is... Hadley, isn't it?"

"Yes!"

"What'm I doing here?"

"Shriekers," said Hadley. "One's got you."

"How're you here?"

"I've got the shrieker," she said.

"It ain't going to take neither of us!"

Gristle closed his eyes and wrinkled his brow. A moment later, Hadley was back in the cave, her body pressed against the spines on the shrieker's back. It thrashed and snapped its teeth at her, but she didn't dare let go. Gristle's eyes focused, then an angry sneer formed on his lip. He raised his hands and took hold of the shrieker's head then thrust his thumbs into the creature's eyes. It howled in pain and let him go. Gristle and Hadley tumbled to the ground where the shrieker lay thrashing and screaming in agony.

"Where're the brownies?" Gristle rose to his feet. When Hadley pointed toward them, he nodded and ran toward Tom. Hadley took the hint and sprinted for Jerry.

To her surprise, the brownie stood unharmed in front of the shrieker, which lay dead on the floor of the cavern.

"How?" She knelt to acknowledge the brownie.

"Well, Miss," said Jerry. "I almost died, and that was the scariest thing that's ever happened to me. But I came to terms with it. I thought I was going to die. So, I suppose, the shrieker just starved."

"What about Tom?"

A look of panic crossed Jerry's face as he climbed onto Hadley's arm. She hurried over to the corner where Gristle was trying to wrench the last shrieker off the brownie with no success.

"Can't... move... its... hand," grunted Gristle.

"What's he afraid of?" She was ready to put her hand back on the shrieker's neck to go back in like she did with Gristle.

"I know," said Jerry as he jumped to the ground. He hurried to Tom's side and chirped into his ear. A series of clicks and bird noises followed. Then, Tom's eyes regained focus and he raised his spear and stabbed the hand that had him. The shrieker howled then looked from one to the next. When its eyes made it to Hadley and saw no fear there, it scurried off into the shadows.

Tom stood with his arms around Jerry's neck.

"What'd you say?" Gristle raised an eyebrow.

"I know what his worst fear is," said Jerry. "It's life without me. The shrieker convinced him I was dead. I just let him know I was here."

"It don't matter what's in the world," said Tom. "So long as we're together, we can face anything."

Chapter Twenty-One

"We've got to be getting close," said Hadley. Her legs wobbled as they walked, a product of too much energy spent and not enough rest. Her head felt too heavy for her neck, and no matter where she looked, her eyes wouldn't focus. But her feet kept moving through the tunnel, guided only by the glowing moss that clung to the walls.

Gristle walked a bit in front, his bow long since lost. Whatever he came up against, he had to rely on the rocks at his feet and his empty hands to deal with it. And while Hadley had her backpack, she couldn't imagine what a bag of salt or iron nails would do against a creature strong enough to warp reality the way the changeling had done.

Well, it didn't really warp reality. It created realistic illusions. Realistic enough to have them wandering through a relatively small patch of woods for days.

She stumbled and fell but caught herself and kept going.

"We need to stop," said Jerry in her ear. "You've got nothing left."

"No," she said. "Grandma's close by. I can feel it. I have to get to them."

"But what if you're too weak to fight?" Tom spoke from her other shoulder. "You can barely walk, much less fight."

"No!" She didn't mean to shout, but she was so tired. "We've come so far! And I want my family back!"

At her last word, she stumbled and fell to the rock floor. Her knee scraped on rough stone, and the brownies jumped before her face struck the floor as well. She lay for a moment. They were right, of course. What could she do? She was just a child, and a tired one at that. Grandma couldn't stop it, and she was so much more powerful than Hadley. Even if she had all of her strength, a full belly, and a nap, she didn't have a prayer of beating the changeling. It all seemed so hopeless.

Angry tears of frustration trickled from her eyes. What she wouldn't give for just a nap, just another apple.

"Miss?" It was Jerry. He and Tom stood hand in hand in front of her. "I know you said no before, but, well, we was thinking. You need a bit of life. And if you was to take both ours, well, maybe—"

"No," she sobbed. "I'm not taking any power out of you. It would kill you both, and I don't want that!"

"Shame you can't take it from the rocks," said Gristle. "This here cave's as old as the dirt itself. No telling how much its seen or how much power, neither."

Through eyes blurred with tears, Hadley stared at Gristle. Could it be so simple? Grandma said everything had a life force to it, its own energy. Trees, grass, animals, *even rocks*. The cave was old, huge by any standard. When she fed her own life energy to Jerry to heal him, she hardly noticed it. But if she took it back, he would die. The rocks, however, were so huge that if she took her fill, there was a good chance the rocks would never even notice the difference. A silly notion or not, it was worth at least a try.

Hadley pushed herself to her feet and wobbled over to the nearest wall. Then, she put her hands on it and closed her eyes. Just like Grandma taught her, she pictured the energy at her center, swirling like a vortex. This time, however, instead of pushing it out she imagined herself drawing inward, pulling the energy from outside.

In her mind, there came a low hum, a rumble that she felt in her gut more than she heard. But the more she pulled, the louder it grew until the rumble became sound, then sound took shape and form. The rocks sang. As they relinquished their energies, her body grew stronger, and the song from the rocks filled her with inexplicable joy.

Hadley opened her eyes to find Gristle, Tom, and Jerry staring at her, their jaws slack. The blue glow of the cave moss was no longer evident on their faces, as some new light, yellow and warm, had taken its place. It took her only a moment to realize the new glow came from her.

When she'd had her fill, she took her hand away. The glow faded, and she stood staring at her own hands with newfound wonder.

"I never seen nothing like that," said Gristle. "Not in all my born days, by the root. Never saw nothing even close."

The brownies said nothing but stood with awestruck looks on their faces.

"The rocks," she said. "Did you hear them singing?"

"Weren't no singing," said Gristle. "Not that I heard."

"Us neither," said Jerry. "All we heard was the drip-drip-drip of water falling off that pointy bit there."

"But they sang to me," she said. "It was the most beautiful sound."

"Maybe it was just for you to hear," said Gristle. "And you alone. But we didn't hear nothing."

"How do you feel, Miss?" Jerry took a tentative step forward.

"Better," she said. "Awake and strong."

"Good," said Gristle. "Better than you was, anywho."

"C'mon," said Hadley. "We're running out of time."

There wasn't anything in particular that made Hadley think that time was running out for her grandmother and brothers. No one set a clock or an ominous-looking hourglass, and no one said anything had to be done by a certain time. But all the same, the longer it took, the more certain she was. She had to get to her family, and soon, if she had any hope of saving them and getting back to Grandma's house.

She reached under her shirt and felt for the silver whistle. It was still where it needed to be, waiting for her to give it a good blast. Then Grandpa would come and lead them out. The iron key would get her back through the veil, and she could spend the rest of her life apologizing to Grandma for breaking the rules and promising her brothers that she loved them.

Gristle walked ahead, but he seemed off somehow, different than he'd been before the shriekers. Before, he was gruff, but there was an undeniable shine of his good heart underneath. But now he seemed more than angry. His eyes darted faster from shadow to shadow, and every sound made him flinch. Reliving his fear hurt him deeply, and she suspected it had taken him a long time to get past it. With the wound picked open again, she wasn't sure how long it would take for him to recover, or if he even would.

The brownies rode on her shoulders, each with their spears at the ready. Tom, she didn't worry about. But Jerry, despite his bravado and courage, was still seriously injured. All she'd managed to do was stop the bleeding and the infection. But it wouldn't take much for him to be finished. And then, where would Tom be? Devastated.

Gristle stopped short and held up a hand, then he turned.

"I don't know if that's real or not," he said. "Look at it through your witch's stone."

What stood in front of her appeared to be nothing more than a simple wooden door. In fact, it looked very much like the front door to Grandma's house, red with heavy iron bands and an iron latch and hinges. Of all the things they'd faced, it seemed strange to her that this door, for all its simplicity, seemed to give her the most anxiety.

She held up the stone and peered through. The door stayed where it sat, as if framed into the stone tunnel. It wasn't an illusion, though. It was real, which meant someone *had* brought it through the cavern and affixed it in place. The only difference was in its condition. Without the stone, the door looked new, the bands black and sturdy.

Through the stone, however, its true age became apparent. The boards warped and split, and the door hung off one hinge at an angle. The bands were made more of rust than iron anymore, and the latch was simply gone.

"It's a door," she said. "It's broken."

"Something got in?" Tom gripped his spear tighter.

"More likely, out," said Gristle. "This is where she hides. Where she's been all these years."

"But that's dumb." Hadley touched the door with her free hand. It was roughhewn, not made by modern equipment. Whoever made it, did so with old tools. "Who would think they could keep her in with just a door? And why?"

"Don't much matter," said Gristle. "Don't look like it did no good."

"Maybe," she said. A simple wooden door didn't make much sense. But then, nothing in her world made much sense since the day she came to Grandma's. Who would believe, much less make sense of, magic or changelings or living shadows or brambles that tried to eat people? The world was wider than she'd ever known, and much of it didn't make sense.

Hadley pulled Grandma's book from her backpack.

"We've got to go," said Gristle. "We ain't got time for—"

"I need to know," she said. "It could be important. Tell me about doorways."

The book shuddered in her hands so violently that she dropped it to the ground. Then, it flipped open and pages fanned past until they stopped on a page with an illustration that looked very much like the door in front of them, but unbroken.

Doorways, it said, *are unique in that they are meant not only to allow things in and out, but to keep things in and out as well. In magic, a threshold can be used as a barrier to separate two worlds, to realms, or even just two rooms. Homes have natural thresholds, but others can be created with remnants of home.*

The door was magical. Whoever put it in the tunnel had doubtless used magic to try to keep the changeling in. But what did it mean, *remnants of home*?

"Fat lot o' good that was," said Gristle. "So the door used to be magic. Now it's nothing but broke and firewood."

"C'mon," said Hadley. "What we're looking for is through here. I can feel it."

Guided by the witch's stone, she maneuvered around the broken pieces of the door and into the cavern beyond.

Chapter Twenty-Two

The air on the other side of the door was colder by a few degrees, enough so that when she breathed out, Hadley's breath was like smoke in the air. As she stepped further in, her skin prickled as if being poked by needles, and the fine hairs at the back of her neck stood up.

"I don't like it here, Miss," said Jerry. "Something here don't feel right."

"Don't you worry," said Tom, though his voice shook and it was obvious his bravado was false. "Nothing we can't handle."

Gristle said nothing, but his pelt looked thicker, wilder. If whatever was in the air was affecting him like it did Hadley, he had a lot more hair to stand up.

"Come in." The voice was Patricia's, the little-girl voice that Hadley knew. But there was a coldness to it, a bitter cruelty she'd not heard before. "So nice you decided to play with me after all."

"Take that skin off!" growled Gristle. "You been wearing it too long! You ain't this child's family, and you knows it!"

"But I've grown accustomed to this look," said the changeling. "It's so small and unassuming. So much tasty sadness to go with it."

"Where's my family?"

"With us," said the changeling. "Don't worry. They're living in a world of my creation now, where they can have everything they love."

"I want them back," said Hadley.

"I thought you'd be happy," said the changeling with an exaggerated pout. "No more sharing time with your annoying brothers. No more chores to do for your grandmother. I can teach you all about magic. You don't need them anymore. You just have to stay with me."

The brownies on her shoulders brandished their spears, which seemed to amuse the changeling. Gristle shifted from foot to foot, paced like an angry dog. But the changeling didn't move. She stood in the same place, hands behind her back, with an infuriating smile on her face. Not even her eyes moved as she spoke.

"That's not her," said Hadley. "That's one of her illusions."

"Smart," said the changeling. "Too smart for your own good. Let's see if you're smart enough for this."

The image of the changeling melted away into the cracks in the stone. Almost immediately, the room shook. The great rock stalactites above cracked and fell to the floor, sending Gristle and the brownies scurrying for their lives. Hadley ran and dodged as great slabs of stone fell and drove her toward one end of the cavern. As another came down, she dove under an outcropping and hugged her knees to her chest and tried to remember to breathe.

The rumble, the sound of the rocks falling, the shouts and screams from her friends, as well as those that came from her, were deafening. She closed her eyes and tried to be as small as possible until the noise died down, and the cavern was quiet again. When she opened her eyes, the blue glow of the moss and plants was all but gone. She choked and coughed as she struggled to breathe against the dust in the air. In the dim light, there was no sign of Gristle, Tom, or Jerry, dead or alive.

"Hello?" she called. "Anybody?"

A ragged cough answered from somewhere far away.

"Here," Gristle said, though his voice was raspy and weak. "Can't see nothing."

"Tom? Jerry?"

"Here, Miss." Jerry's voice was small, at least as far away as Gristle's.

Hadley crawled out of her hiding place and tried to see through the dust-filled air. The moss still glowed, but it did little good. Instead of seeing the cavern and her friends, the only thing in front of her was a sheet of blue grey.

"Have to wait it out," said Gristle. "Too much in the air. It's dangerous, trying to find each other in this fog."

She hated to admit it, but he was right. The only thing she could realistically do was hide in her hole until the dust settled and hope not to choke to death in the meantime. She pulled her shirt up over her mouth and nose, then felt her way back under the outcropping and waited.

"Tom?" The other two answered, but he had not. "Where are you?"

There was no answer. After a few moments of silence, the air was filled with quick trills and whistles as Jerry called out to his partner in their native tongue. He, too, was met with silence.

"Miss!" Jerry's voice was frantic. "I can't find him nowhere! Where's he gone?"

A thousand images flooded her mind. He could've been hiding or injured. Or worse. He could be dead or taken by the changeling. No matter the case, all they could do was sit in the blue-gray fog and wait.

"I don't know," she said. "We have to wait. When we can see, we'll find him."

"But what if it's too late by then?"

She didn't have an answer. All she had was dread and a feeling that the worst had happened in her gut.

Without the ability to see, Hadley also lost her ability to judge time. Every tiny noise echoed in the blue-grey fog, and her imagination, deprived of visual stimulus, created the most horrible creatures from which they came. She wished she could read Grandma's book, or play a game, or do anything to make the time pass faster. But all she could do was sit and wait.

After a time, she looked up to see that some of the grey was gone and shadows had become evident.

"Not long now," she said. "I can see shapes."

"Yeah," said Gristle. "Still can't figure out where I am."

Below Gristle's voice and her own, there was a soft low murmur of Jerry's chirps and tweets so mournful they could only be his prayer for the life of his partner.

She took a few tentative steps but stumbled in the rubble. Better, she thought, to crouch and feel her way around.

"Keep talking," she called out. "So I can find you."

Gristle's voice became a constant barrage of complaints and swears as he kicked rocks with his bare feet. Jerry's tweets and clicks became a low murmur she could understand.

"By the root, by the soil, let him be alive." He repeated the phrase over and over.

As she moved through the debris, the clouds cleared a bit until she could see the rest of the room. Gristle, Jerry, and Tom were nowhere to be seen. But where they'd been was a wall of rubble.

"Gristle! Are you there?"

"I'm here," he said. "By the root, I'm here."

She traced the wall until she found a small opening, large enough for only a brownie. Gristle peered through.

"Ain't no way I'm getting through this," he said. "But..."

He lifted his hand to the hole. In it, Tom lay motionless.

"Is he..?"

"Breathing," said Gristle. "Looks like he took a nasty knock."

"He found him?" Jerry's voice jolted her with its proximity. He scrambled up the jagged pile of rocks as best as he could. Hadley scooped him up and placed him at the hole.

"Go," she said. "Take care of him. I'll try to find my family."

"You can't go alone!" Gristle glared through the hole. "She'll eat you alive!"

"I don't have a choice," said Hadley. "I can't get back through to you, and you can't get to me."

"Blow that whistle thing you got 'bout your neck!"

If she blew the whistle, Grandpa would come and whisk them away, but if she blew it before she found the others, they'd be lost. She'd have to try to find the lair all over again, and what if, when she found it, he changeling had moved it and they were never to be seen again? The image of the graves in the graveyard replayed in her mind.

"I can't," she said. "Not until I find them. Get Tom and Jerry out and back to their people. Thank you for helping me get this far."

"But..."

"I couldn't have gotten this far without you," she said. "All of you. Now, please, get out of here. Let me find my family."

Gristle nodded and then reached as far as he could through the rock wall. Hadley did the same until their fingertips touched. She let the moment linger for a moment then pulled away, turned her back to the hole, and moved toward where she'd last seen Patricia.

She had to remind herself that the changeling wasn't really Patricia, or even a human girl for that matter. It was... well, she didn't know. The picture in Grandma's book showed a creature that had no real shape, but she found it hard to believe. It also said that they were adept at illusions, but the fallen rocks were real enough. When she got out, *if* she got out, she had a few entries of her own to put in the old book. Or maybe for her own.

CHAPTER TWENTY-THREE

*O*nce upon a time, went the story Mom used to tell her. *There was a little girl who got lost in the woods.*

For her entire life, she'd assumed the story was made up, a fairy tale. The story always had monsters and brownies, and it always had a happy ending. But it wasn't made up. At least, most of it wasn't. The happy ending was complete fiction. But the little girl that got lost in the woods was real.

And today, Hadley was that little girl.

As she searched the cave, she made it to the spot where the changeling stood. Behind the spot was a rock, massive and out of place. It didn't look like the rest of the cavern. It was darker, more jagged than the rest of the stone that surrounded her. She circled the rock until she found her way behind it. There, just out of view, was an opening just large enough for someone her size, or Patricia's, to fit through. Beyond the opening, the tunnel was darker than night, and her breath froze as it came out of her mouth. It had to be the way to the changeling.

She took a frigid breath, placed a hand on the wall to feel her way, and crept into the opening.

The darkness pressed in around her like a living thing made of cold jelly, wet and oppressive. In the black, a faint hissing sound grew stronger, turned to whispers and words that she couldn't understand.

Her outstretched fingers guided her through the hallway, dragging across smooth rocks and crevices worn deep with time, until she came to a bend. As she rounded it, there came a light at the end of the tunnel. Not bright, not even so much that it chased away the wet cold, but enough so she could see. She hurried through the opening and into a larger chamber.

In the center of the chamber, roots hung down from above, a vast network from one of the larger trees in the forest. Were she to judge by the size of the roots, the tree had to be bigger even than the Black Elder. Strands like tendrils snaked into the darkness, found their ways into the cracks in the walls. Bound within the knotted roots were her brothers and grandmother.

"Josh! Cole!" She ran as close as she dared. "Grandma!"

They hung in the roots, flies trapped in a web. Their eyes were open and sightless, their jaws slack. She jumped and waved her arms in front of them, shouted their names, but they didn't respond.

"They are mine," said a cold voice. "They will not hear you unless I allow it."

The changeling hung from the roots just as did the others. But where they were cocooned, the roots dug into the changeling's skin so it was difficult to tell where the tree ended and the creature began. As it slowly lowered to the floor, Hadley shuddered. It still wore a sweet face, its white dress unmarred. Even in the cavern, it still held the image of the little girl, too perfect, too clean. Not for the first time, Hadley wondered what the creature actually looked like. The book couldn't tell her, said no one knew. But it didn't deserve to wear her mother's sister's face. She wanted to look at the face in the photos and regard them with love, not with the pain the creature inflicted. It was time to find out what the changeling really looked like without illusions, once and for all.

Hadley took the witches stone from her pocket and held it up. With the illusions stripped away, she saw the changeling for what it really was.

It no longer held the appearance of a little girl. Gone were the blonde ringlets, the white dress, the pale skin with rosy cheeks. In its place was a creature with huge, lamplike eyes and a bald scalp. Its sallow skin reflected what little light was in the room to reveal scales across its spindly arms and legs. The creature's wet mouth seemed far too wide to fit in its head, and when it spoke, jagged points of teeth looked ready to mutilate its lips.

"Patricia?"

"It's as good a name as any," said the creature. "Though it is far better suited to a different shape."

It shuddered, and its bones seemed to collapse in upon the thing as it twisted and reformed. When it stood again, it looked like the little girl Hadley had met in the woods.

"Let them go," said Hadley. "Please!"

"Why should I?"

"They're my family!"

"Oh?" roared Patricia. "Am I not? Are we not summer sisters?"

"You're a monster!"

"That's what the other one said." Her smile grew wider and her eyes wider. "When she complained about her sister, I took her. When she wanted her back, I took her place. I did everything that one wanted, and still she called me a monster! Then they bound me in place here! But I got out!"

Mom. The changeling was talking about Mom and her sister, Patricia. The *real* Patricia. It made sense now. Her mother's guilt, the refusal to teach magic, that she never mentioned her little sister. She still blamed herself.

Just like Hadley still blamed herself for the death of her father.

But it wasn't Mom's fault either. Every kid complained about their little brother or sister. That didn't mean they really wanted them gone. Not *really* really.

"I want them back," said Hadley. "You can't just take them."

"I can do what I want!" shouted the creature. Her limbs stretched and her jaw unhinged, and the angrier she grew, the less she was able to hold the illusion of the little girl.

Hadley reached into her shirt and grabbed for the silver whistle. As she raised it to her lips, a root shot out from beneath the tree and ensnared her wrist. Another snaked forward and ensnared her waist. It pulled and jerked, then slowly lifted her off the ground.

"You're not leaving," said Patricia. "You'll never leave. You're going to stay with me for the rest of your short life!"

A high-pitched scream pierced the air. The changeling's head snapped in the direction of the sound, only to be met by the spear held by Jerry as he leaped through the air. Had she not turned, the spear might have hit her cheek, graced the creature's face. But she turned so quickly, so completely, that the tip of the spear went straight into the pupil of the changeling's eye.

She screamed and clawed at the shaft of wood that protruded from the ruined orb. As she did, her control on the roots faltered, and the root at Hadley's wrist loosened. She gave the silver whistle one long solid blast.

The cavern lit up in white light so bright it hurt Hadley's eyes. In the center, a smoky whirlwind spiraled. She expected Grandpa to step out, but it wasn't him.

"Mom?"

Her mother stood, angry and defiant, at the eye of the storm. The wind whipped her hair and put her business-casual clothes to flapping.

"You took my sister." Mom's voice echoed through the cavern. "And you try to take my *daughter*? You try to take my *mother* and my *sons*?

She ducked her head and pulled her shoulders in tight as she drew power from all around her. Then, with a single step forward, she screamed and let go of every ounce of energy she'd drawn. The air in front of her rippled with heat as it struck the changeling fully. At its touch, the creature's skin burned.

The changeling screamed and writhed on the ground as pieces of its stolen skin flaked away, revealing the beast beneath.

"Hurry," said Mom. "That won't stop her for long."

The roots that held Grandma and the twins drooped and slowly lowered them to the ground. Hadley ran to their sides, but none of them woke up.

"Help me," said Mom. She took Grandma by the shoulders and dragged her out of the chamber, through the tunnel, and out into the room where the stalactites fell. Hadley took one of the boys and followed. When she ran back for Cole, she found Jerry trying to pull him.

"He's a heavy one, isn't he, Miss?"

Hadley scooped him up and put him on her shoulder, then she took her brothers by the arms and dragged him out of the chamber as well.

"Quickly," said Mom. "We need to make a threshold."

"I don't know how," said Hadley. "The book, it said I needed a remnant of home, and I don't even know what that means."

"Who packed your backpack?"

"Grandpa."

"Give it to me!" Mom took it and peered inside. After a moment of rummaging, her face lit up. "Aha!" she said as she raised the bag of red brick dust out of the pack.

"Brick dust?"

"From the bricks used to build Grandma's chimney," said Mom. "It's a remnant of home. Now we just need to get to the door."

From within the chamber, the changeling roared.

Hadley dashed toward the hole in the wall where Gristle and she had said goodbye. It was still too small for her to get through.

"What can we do?" she wailed.

"Hold onto your brother and me," said Mom. "And close your eyes."

Hadley did as she was told. Mom murmured something under her breath, then the air around her grew to blisteringly hot.

"Mom?" she called without opening her eyes.

There was a *pop*, then pain. It felt like she imagined it would to be turned wrong side out and then back again. The pain started as a dull ache in her bones, then it felt like every bone broke at once. Her skin felt like it did when she accidently stabbed herself with a thumbtack, but all over. The sensation happened all at once in a single breath, then her legs gave out under her and she fell to the floor. When she opened her eyes, she was on the other side of the wall.

She was about to ask how, but her stomach twisted, and she heaved bile onto the nearby rocks.

"Come on," said Mom. "We have to get back through that door."

Behind them, the howls of the changeling grew louder, more angry and desperate. When it reached the hole in the wall, it screamed.

"Hadley!"

She turned and stared through the hole. The creature's good eye burned with rage as it pressed its face to the edge of the hole, then it shifted and ebbed until it slid into the hole like a snake.

"I'll play with you forever!" it hissed.

Mom dragged Grandma while Hadley took each of the boys' arms and pulled as hard as she could. The door was only a few feet away. If they could just make it past, Mom could fix everything.

Mom got Grandma through the doorway and left her propped against the stone wall. Then, she turned back and took the boys from Hadley and dragged them as well. Hadley ran to keep up. As they passed through the door-way, Mom stopped and turned.

"This remnant of home," she said. "A threshold make. Protect both sides, for goodness sake." Mom poured the bag of red brick dust across the line of the doorway. As the last bit fell, the changeling slithered to the doorway. It slammed against the empty doorway as if blocked by the old wooden door.

"No!" it screamed. "Let me out! Let me out!"

"Come on," said Mom.

"Wait," said Hadley. She stepped as close to the threshold as she dared. "Why? Why did you steal my family? Why did you destroy Gristle's people? Why?"

"Because," said her mother from behind her. "It is in its nature to do so. You can't blame a dog for being a dog. It does what it does because it is in its nature to do so. You can't blame it for being what it is."

Hadley took one last look at the nightmarish vision of the creature banging on a wall of solid air, then she pushed the old door toward the frame. It wouldn't close, but at least it could obscure enough of the changeling that she didn't have to see it. Then she knelt beside her mother, grandmother, and brothers, and breathed deeply for the first time in days.

CHAPTER TWENTY-FOUR

Grandma stood at the stove cooking, almost like nothing had happened. She stirred the pot and hummed quietly then tasted the stew, nodded, and stirred some more. Grandpa's ghost sat at the dining table, a smile on his face. Josh and Cole were upstairs in their room, still asleep.

Hadley slowly climbed the stairs to the second floor. Mom's old room stood open, and light poured from within. She went to the doorway and looked inside.

Mom sat on the bed, a photograph in her hands. Tears ran down one of her cheeks.

"Mom?"

"Hi, sweetie," said Mom. "C'mon in."

"Why didn't you ever tell me?" Hadley sat down on the bed next to her mother.

"Because," said mom. "I was ashamed. I thought it was my fault."

"But it wasn't," said Hadley.

"I know that now," said Mom. "Just like it wasn't your fault your father died. It was tragic, but there's nothing you could've done to stop it."

Hadley nodded. It didn't take the hurt away, but it made it better somehow, like maybe she could heal someday.

"What about Patri— the changeling?"

"I don't know," said Mom. "She took Patricia a long time ago."

"Thing like that never dies," said Grandma from the doorway. "Too old. All it does is get more and more angry."

"How're you feeling?" Hadley couldn't look her in the eyes. Whether the changeling was her fault or not, she still broke the rules, and that was what let the creature in the house.

"Better," said Grandma. "Thank you. Y'all need to get downstairs. There's folk here who want to see you."

Hadley and her mother exchanged glances then got up and headed for the door.

"By the way," said Mom. "You haven't seen my diary, have you? I can't find it."

"It's in my room," said Hadley. "I just wanted to know about what you were like when you lived here."

"I don't mind," said Mom. "Just put it back when you're done with it."

At the bottom of the stairs, Hadley turned to see Gristle in the kitchen doorway. He fidgeted and looked around nervously, gave terse but polite answers as Grandma spoke to him. On the table, Tom and Jerry sat on stools made of thread spools.

"Gristle! Tom! Jerry!" Hadley hurried to Gristle's side and hugged him.

"No hugging!" growled the puckwudgie. "I'm against hugging!"

"Too bad," giggled Hadley. Then, she hurried to the table and tried to gently hug the brownies. "This is my mom."

Gristle bowed a little. The brownies stood and bowed deeply.

"Thank you," said Mom, "for helping my daughter."

"Yes," said Grandma. "And for not letting so many years of prejudice come between us."

"Meh," said Gristle. "I known about this house for a long time. Always heard you was alright. For *people*."

"And I know your name too," said Grandma. "Someone a long time ago said that you couldn't be trusted, but I never believed it. Glad to see it's not true."

"Well," said Gristle, after an awkward silence. "Guess I'd better be on my way. Stuff to do."

"Like what?" Hadley put her hands on her hips.

"Uh, you know." Gristle dug a toe at the floor as if he could dig it up. "Stuff."

"Join us," said Grandma. "For supper. It's not puckwudgie food, but I figure it'll do you some good."

"It does smell good," said Gristle. "Don't mind if I do."

As they sat at the table and dished up helpings of Grandma's stew, it occurred to Hadley how strange it was that Grandma just happened to have dishes and utensils the size for brownies in her cabinet or that Mom saw Grandpa without a problem. Everything seemed perfect. Too much so. Something was wrong.

"Jerry," she said. "How're you feeling?"

"Fine, Miss," he smiled.

"But you almost died."

"Your Grandma," he said. "Fine medicines, she has."

"Mom? You can see Grandpa now?"

"Of course," said her mother. "Why wouldn't I be able to see him?"

"Because he's dead," she said. "This isn't real. None of this is real."

"Sweetie?" Worry crossed her mother's face, but beneath it was something else, darker. "Of course this is real. What are you talking about."

"It's not real!" Hadley turned and ran up the stairs to the second floor. Mom's room was just as she'd left it, and she'd known about the diary because Hadley knew about it. But just like the wrong house, there were things she didn't know, doors she'd never opened.

She gripped the first doorknob and tried to turn it. Locked.

"Hadley!" Grandma stood at the top of the stairs with her hands on her hips. "I told you not to go in locked rooms!"

"Why?" yelled Hadley. "What's in this one? Unlock it and show me!"

"What's gotten into you?" Her mother stomped her foot. "You're behaving like a little beast!"

"What's gotten into *you*? You've never used that phrase in your entire life! None of this is real!"

She threw her shoulder at the closed door. Wood splintered and the door opened inward. Hadley's momentum left her suspended in black nothing. Slowly, her body turned to face the doorway, where her mother stood fuming.

"Now look what you've done!" Her mother's body twisted and reshaped until Patricia stood in the doorway. "I did everything! I made the perfect world for you! It was a world where your stupid friends could live with your stupid family! Why couldn't you just be happy and play with me?"

The changeling threw her arms down and, with them, the walls of the house crumbled. What didn't tumble to the ground faded like smoke until at last Hadley could see the real world. Her grandmother and brothers still hung suspended in the roots of the tree. Alongside of them were Gristle, Tom, and Jerry. The vines that ensnared her arms before she blew the whistle withered and crumbled to dust, dropping her to the ground.

"I can give them everything," said Patricia. "Right now, they're living in their perfect worlds. Think about it! If you wake them up, you'll be stealing their happiness away!"

"But it's not real!"

"Real?" the changeling laughed. "Real is pain! They could've lived out the rest of their lives in blissful slumber. Instead, they're going to die screaming!"

"But why?"

"You cannot blame me for what I am," said the changeling. "This is how I feed! Whomever I ensnare, I take their remaining years and add them to my own."

"That's horrible!" Hadley's horror mixed with anger at the thought of her family, her new friends, dropped into a fantasy world while the creature drained their lives away. The mixture burned in her heart and bubbled like a cauldron as the raw power inside of her swirled and thrashed. The creature wore the face of her mother's sister, enslaved her friends, and still asked her to stay and play?

"Wake up!" She didn't mean to let go of the anger in her, gave no command to loose all the energy inside. But when she shouted, the command came out in a visible wave of white light. The energy of the rocks, the anger, the love she felt for her friends and family, all poured out of her in a searing hot blast. Wherever it touched, the tree writhed and withered, turned to ash and embers, then dropped its captives to the ground.

"No!" shrieked the changeling. "They're mine! They're all mine!"

Before Hadley's unbelieving eyes, the creature's form shifted and ebbed from the little girl disguise to something with less shape, then to another puckwudgie. It flowed, liquid tar, into the shape of a tree, then to a fox, then a bear, then it fell to the ground, its breath coming in ragged gasps.

The creature in front of her was the changeling's true shape, just as it had been when it was revealed to her earlier.

But as she watched, the scales on its arms flaked and peeled, the spines cracked. Its eyes went milky, and deep wrinkles formed in its hide.

"NO!" it wailed. "You can't! No! They're mine! They're all mine!"

The others stirred, groaned, and sat up one by one. Gristle pushed himself to standing on wobbly legs.

"Where..? I was with Lum. She was..."

"It wasn't real," said Hadley, though it hurt her to do so. "It was *her*. She put you there so you wouldn't feel it when she killed you."

"Kill you all..." muttered the changeling as its form shriveled. "Swallow you all..."

"Come on," said Hadley as she raised the silver whistle to her lips. "Time to go."

She blew a mighty blast.

CHAPTER TWENTY-FIVE

The pot on the stove sat empty. Grandma sat in her chair, exhausted. The twins sat on the couch, too tired to move but afraid to be alone in their room. Grandpa's ghost wore a worried expression by the fireplace, his body dim in exhaustion. He'd used a lot of his own energy, and it would take time and rest for him to look solid again. In the light from the fire, Gristle sat. Beside him, Tom and Jerry nursed their wounds, courtesy of medicine provided by Grandma. No one spoke or even looked at each other. And for it, Hadley felt terrible, too.

It had to be done if they were to be saved. The changeling would've eaten them, drained them away to husks and used their remaining years to extend her reign. But to save them, she had to pull them out of their greatest fantasies, their perfect worlds.

"D'you think it's dead?" Cole spoke without looking up.

"No," said Grandma. "Creature like that won't die. It'll just hide for a while. But it won't die."

"You mean it'll come back for us?" Josh's voice shook as he spoke.

"No," said Grandpa. "It won't be back for a long time—if it comes back at all. Don't you worry."

"I'm sorry," said Hadley. "For everything. I'm the one that let it in. I'm the one who broke the rules. And I'm the one who pulled you out of your dream worlds."

"I was with my Lum," said Gristle, his voice choked. "We was happy, with our little'uns."

"I'm so sorry," said Hadley.

"It weren't real," said Gristle. "I knowed it. Lum and my little'uns, they been dead a long time. But part of me didn't care."

"I'm so—"

"You did me a kindness," he said. "Pulling me out of there. It hurts, but I get to live. So thanks."

"From us too," said Tom, his hand and Jerry's intertwined. "I'd rather live with hurt in the real world than without in one of that monster's tricks."

"I think you did just fine," said Grandma. "Not many could go up against a changeling and keep their skins."

"Yeah," said Hadley. "Well, none of it wouldn't happen if I hadn't broken the rules, and I'm sorry."

Grandma looked up and smiled.

"Some of the best things that happen to us, the ones that teach us the most, come from breaking a rule or two," she said. "So long as you learned something, I suppose you can be forgiven."

"I did," said Hadley. "And it won't happen again."

"It will," said Grandma with a wink. "That's part of learning. And I see you made some new friends in the process."

Gristle stood and bowed.

"Aye," he said. "She has."

"The three of you are welcome here," she said. "The veil will allow you to come and go as you please. I'll see to it."

"Thank you," said Jerry.

"Now you boys," said Grandma. "Next summer, you can begin your lessons in magic. If, that is, you want to come back. After what you've been through, I wouldn't blame you if you didn't."

"Are you kidding?" Cole's head snapped up. "This was the best summer ever!"

"We were terrified," said Josh. "We got kidnapped! There was magic and monsters! It wasn't boring!"

"And you?" Grandma leveled her sparkling eyes at Hadley. "Do you think you'll be back? There's so much more for you to learn. But there are more creatures out there in the woods than you know."

She thought for a moment. Yes, it was the most terrifying summer she'd ever had. But then she looked from the faces of Tom and Jerry to Gristle, to her brothers, and smiled. It was worth it.

Lights flashed in the front window and brought the illusion of daylight to darkness. An engine revved, and brakes squealed as gravel crunched. The engine cut off with the slam of a car door.

"Hadley! Boys!"

Hurried steps hit the porch like thunder, and Mom burst through the front door, her eyes wild with panic.

"They're fine," said Grandma without looking up.

"What're you doing here?" Hadley rose to her feet. It looked like Mom, sure. But could she be sure?

Mom flung herself across the space between them and crushed Hadley in a giant hug. She breathed in deep. There was no mistaking the scent, the familiar embrace. It was Mom for real.

"I heard a voice," she sobbed. "And it was you. And you were calling for me. And I woke up, and I knew it was real. I just knew it. I drove all night."

"Yes," said Hadley. "But we're okay. All of us."

Mom pulled away to give her a solid look up and down.

"You're hurt," she said. "What happened?"

"I'm fine," said Hadley. "It was Patricia."

Mom dropped her hands as the color drained from her face.

"Where did you hear that name?"

"She came back." Grandma rose from her chair. "And it's still not your fault."

Mom slumped onto the couch, her expression unreadable.

"It's okay," said Hadley. "Look. Everyone's fine."

"Your daughter did you proud," said Gristle. At his voice, Mom's head snapped toward him as if seeing him for the first time, then her eyes grew large.

"What..? What..?"

"Mom," said Hadley. "This is Gristle. He helped me. He's a friend. And this is Tom and Jerry."

The brownies stood hand-in-hand and bowed deeply to her.

Mom looked from the Folk to Grandma, then to Hadley.

"I'll put a kettle on," said Grandma. "This'll take some explaining."

EPILOGUE

It went better than Hadley expected. Mom listened as everyone told their part. By the time they were finished, it was well past midnight. Grandma insisted everyone stay the rest of the night. Exhaustion left everyone too tired to argue. Gristle curled up under one of Grandma's crochet blankets on the couch while Tom and Jerry held each other in a box with a dishtowel for a cushion.

Hadley helped Grandma put away the dishes before saying goodnight and heading up to her room. At the landing to the second floor, she stopped. The door to Mom's childhood room stood open. Mom sat on the bed, the picture of her sister in her hands.

"I'd convinced myself it wasn't real," she said. "That when Patricia died, it was my fault. I haven't even said her name out loud since before you were born."

"Mom..."

"My magic all but died. I couldn't remember how it felt or how to use it. So, I brought you here. Grandma's the best teacher I know."

"Why didn't you tell me before? About any of it?"

"Would you have believed me?"

Hadley considered. Magic, the Folk, changelings. She had a hard time believing it, even after all she'd been through.

"Probably not," she said. "So, what happens now?"

"That's up to you," said Mom. "What do you want to do?"

"I want to keep learning," she said. "It's scary, but I love it."

"So did I," said her mother. "I felt like I lost a part of myself when my magic went away. And it's taken me years to get back to feeling even a little normal."

Hadley pulled the witches stone from her pocket and peered through the hole. Mom glowed. Not as brightly as Grandma or even herself, but there was a shimmer about her.

"It didn't go away," she said. "It's still there. Maybe you can learn to use it again."

"No," said Mom with a smile. "Whatever's left, it's a ghost of what it used to be. It's for you now. You and your brothers. They're going to be a handful."

She kissed her mother goodnight and climbed the stairs to the third floor. Outside her brothers' door, Hadley listened. Instead of the unsettling quiet came soft snores and the occasional mumble of dreams. She smiled and went into her own room and softly closed the door.

Even though the bed called to her, she didn't want to sleep. Not just yet. If she let go too soon, if she went to sleep, she might wake up and find out that all the nightmares, the Folk, the magic, were just a dream. Hadley walked out onto the reading balcony and looked out across the silver moonlit yard to the tree line. Hadley took the witches stone from her pocket and turned it over in her fingers. A single summer vacation, and nothing would ever be the same. She held the witches stone up and looked through the hole.

The woods were alive with magic.

ACKNOWLEDGEMENTS

The author would like to express his undying thanks for unwavering support and friendship to Nikki, Ward, Wes, and Jake Hopeman; to Mike Arnzen and N.D. Peeler; to Kristin Dearborn and Lucy Snider; to Tim Waggoner and Gary Braunbeck; to Jonathan Papernick and Lisa Dierks; to all the faculty, staff, students, and alumni at both Seton Hill University and Emerson College; to Clint, Heather, Cal, Corbin, and Hadley McCrocklin; to Matt and Meg Taylor; and to Steve "Uncle Creepy" Barton and Danielle Martin—You are my found family. Without you, without your encouragement, this book might never have come to be.

To C.R. Langille and the rest of the Timber Ghost Press crew, thank you for your belief and friendship. We weirdos have to stick together, y'know?

And finally, to Katie, Anna, ZJ, Becky, Blas, Tyler, Hannah, Katie P., Noah, Austin, and Sawyer; to my mom and dad; to my brother, his wife, and his children, all my love and all my thanks. Without you, there would be no me.

About the Author

Scott A. Johnson is the Texas-based author of twelve horror novels, a short story collection, a chapbook, and three true ghost story guides. He has an MFA from Emerson college in writing and publishing popular fiction and teaches in both Emerson's and Seton Hill University's Writing Popular Fiction MFA programs. When he's not figuring out ways to terrify, he spends his time functioning as a father and husband, and riding his motorcycle through the Texas hill country with his pug. For more information, visit his website at http://www.creepylittlebastard.com.

If you enjoyed, *Through the Witches Stone*, please consider leaving a review on Amazon or Goodreads. Reviews help the author and the press.

If you go to www.timberghostpress.com you can sign up for our newsletter so you can stay up-to-date on all our upcoming titles, plus you'll get informed of new horror flash fiction and poetry featured on our site monthly.

Take care and thanks for reading, *Through the Witches Stone* by Scott A. Johnson.

-Timber Ghost Press